Wretched Excess

Wretched Excess

Wickedly Wry Tales

C. Robert Holloway

To order additional copies of this book, contact:
Xlibris Corporation
1-888-795-4274
www.Xlibris.com
Orders@Xlibris.com
72518

Contents

The Inheritance

Chance, ambition, and a loathing for cold weather drove me to live in West Hollywood, California, on and off, for 40 some years—30 of them in a rent-controlled apartment building named "El Mirador," one of those Spanish-villa-like complexes built in the 1920s to house actors lured from Broadway to appear in silent films. Exactly how the promise of living in an ersatz Castilian castle convinced a sophisticated New York stage personality that he or she would feel at home never made any sense to me, but who was I to question so charming an urban legend? Shortly after I moved in, an architect friend dubbed the building, "The Puerto Rican Wedding Cake." A recent drive through the old neighborhood recalled his campy sobriquet, all the more memorable for its political incorrectness.

The charm of cast-plaster ceilings, carved archways, bricked-over fireplaces and hardwood floors, worn thin from decades of sanding and refinishing, offset the paucity of electrical outlets, thumping radiators in January, lack of A/C in July, warped and leaking windows and frequently clogged sinks and toilets. Nevertheless, El Mirador's wonderfully affordable, municipally legislated annual rent increases of 2% are sorely missed.

During those halcyon years, I labored variously as an actor's agent, an assistant to a personal manager, sold bar

7

glass sets door-to-door, co-wrote, produced and directed a waiver-theatre production which won rave reviews, a spate of awards and, despite a seven month run, never earned a nickel. Following that *succès d'estime*, I worked as a location scout and manager and eventually became a production designer for commercials, TV movies and a few feature films.

That work enabled me to meet a number of celebrities—actors, directors, writers, producers and designers—several on their way up—a few rejoicing at the top, the majority drifting laterally and a handful on their mortifying slide down.

One evening, while attending the annual Stuntmen's Prosthesis Banquet, I was approached (cruised is more to the truth) by a handsome older man with a clipped English accent, who turned out to be the legendary press-agent, Geoffrey Putnam. Shortly after introducing himself, Mr. Putnam recited his client list for me—mostly women, a few men, all "first tier," he assured me as he gave me his card and urged me to call. "We'll do lunch. 'L'Orangerie,' Tuesday week."

What the hell? He was charming, sophisticated, obviously connected—I might learn something. And he'd be picking up the tab at a 4 star restaurant I had never been to.

As a result of that elegantly pricey meal, I became one of his favorites, mercifully never having to conjugate the verb with him. It was obvious how much Geoffrey loved his profession for he worked long hours and was not easily reachable as he refused to have an answering machine at home. "Entirely too rude," he condemned the device, so I learned to charm Robbie, his secretary and leave detailed messages at his office.

Geoffrey (never just "Geoff") frequently invited me to his premieres and the parties that followed, several of which he gave at his Doheny Towers penthouse. Despite its location on the east side of Doheny, he referred to it as "My Beverly Hills digs," which technically it wasn't as the dividing line between B.H. and WeHo runs down the middle of the street. When reminded of this, he begrudgingly revised it to "The brink of Beverly Hills."

Having extolled the virtues of his 'brilliant' clients to carefully-selected media members, put a shine on their latest misdeeds and peccadilloes, then bid everyone 'Goodnight,' Geoffrey would pour himself a snifter of Courvoisier, swirl it in his palm and look about mischievously. "Well! Now, that it's just us girls," he declared, in a passable Bette Davis imitation, "Who wants to hear the latest?"

So went the ritual, and soon the dirt surrounding Hollywood royalty and their minions was flying faster than any vacuum could possibly suck up. Always wicked, often witty, rarely cruel, nobody could top Geoffrey in the variety and scope of his tabloidish tales. He frequently referred to his subjects as "BCs," and we'd all giggle, as if we knew what it meant, but I don't think any of us did. I certainly didn't.

At one such Saturday night party, three of his 'cadre,' myself included, drank to excess and since Geoffrey never served food of any kind, ("Canapés make fat! Look at Shelley Winters, for God's sake!") we were too drunk to drive and too poor to call a taxi, so the three of us spent the night—two in his bed and I on the Lazy-boy in his study. At dawn, my well-deserved hangover prodded me awake, sending me stumbling to the bathroom for a lengthy pee and dry heaves.

Exhausted, I returned to peruse the memorabilia blanketing his walls and while contemplating a plaster replica of Michelangelo's *David*, spied a folder that had fallen behind it, retrieved it and couldn't resist untying its ribbon. It contained a diploma from FDR High School in Shamokin Dam, Pennsylvania made out to 'Robert Ernst Putzdorf, Esq.' along with a VFW debating team certificate issued at *Penn State University, Harrisburg.*

So much for Geoffrey's claims of a childhood spent on the Isle of Jersey among landed English gentry. I retied the ribbon and carefully replaced the folder. Later that morning, over black coffee, Geoffrey indicated his displeasure at my having spent the night in his study, away from his watchful eye.

It wasn't until years later, when I visited him at Cedars Sinai, oxygen nodules jammed in his nose, forearms pierced with syringes conveying God knows what into his veins, I summoned the courage to ask him point-blank, "What does 'BC' mean?"

"Oh, dear boy. I'm so disappointed. I thought finally, you were going to tell me you love me," he whispered.

"Well, that too," was all I could muster.

A nurse entered the room, took his pulse and temperature, scribbled a few notes on her clipboard and turned up the valve on the oxygen. After she left, Geoffrey signaled for me to approach.

"Dear Boy. BC stands for . . ." his voice trailed off as the hiss of the oxygen increased. He struggled to speak. "BC . . . shit! I can't believe you're so dumb." His look of chagrin became one of pain. He turned away, his body convulsed for a moment and then he stopped breathing. I frantically pushed the signal button and shouted for the nurse but it was too late. After three decades of dominating the Hollywood PR scene, Geoffrey Putnam was gone. And with him, the definitive answer to my question.

An impressive throng of screen, television and theatre folk showed up for his tastefully-austere funeral at the Beverly Hills Unitarian church, including several clients on walkers and wheelchairs. I couldn't help wondering which among them were his BCs, but didn't think it an appropriate time to ask.

Rumors flew that Geoffrey's lawyers were able to locate but one surviving relative, an octogenarian Aunt, sequestered at the Shamokin Dam Alzheimer's Haven. Shortly, his estate was swamped in a tide of delinquent taxes, legal fees and payoffs to a pair of celebrated male escorts who'd threatened to tell all to *The Star* and *National Enquirer*.

Nearly a year passed when I received a call from a man named Deutsch, claiming to be one of Geoffrey's executors. "We were clearing out Mr. Putnam's personal effects," he whispered in conspiratorial tones, "when we came across a manuscript that appears to be for a book he was contemplating." He followed this revelation with a profound silence which I finally broke.

"And?"

"Would you care to pick it up at our office? Save the estate a few bucks, or, if you have a FedEx account, give me the number and we can overnight it to you."

"I don't understand, Sir. What does this have to do with me?"

"Thought I told you. There's a post-it on the cover. In Putnam's handwriting. Says, 'Give to Holloway. Likes macabre. Maybe he can edit.'"

"Geoffrey never mentioned any such thing to me."

"Far as we can tell, you're the only Holloway he knew."

"That may be. Is there a date on it?"

"No! Putnam never dated anything! What's the date matter, anyway? Look, I haven't got all day. You want it or don't you?" His cackle was laced with anything but humor. "For all you know, it might be worth a fortune."

"Yeah, and for all you know, it isn't."

"What's that supposed to mean?"

"Never mind. Is your firm willing to give me a release stating the manuscript is mine to do with as I wish, no strings attached?"

"Jesus, you're hard. I'll have to get back to you on that one."

I started to say, "You have my number," when he slammed the receiver down.

Over a month passed before I heard from Deutsch again. This time he was all unction and couldn't convey his message fast enough. "My associates have determined that Mr. Putnam intended for you to look over the manuscript with the possibility of collaboration. Obviously, he is no longer able to pursue that goal. Therefore, as sole executor, our firm has elected to bequeath the manuscript to you, in its entirety, without prejudice."

"Thank you! Along with a signed and notarized document that states all that unequivocally?"

Despite cupping his hand over his receiver, I heard him relay, "This guy's a fuckin' pain in the ass." Then, to me, dripping with condescension, "Yes, we'll give you the release. Now you want this thing or don't you?"

"Where are you located?"

"Century City—1600 Avenue of the Stars—30ᵗʰ floor."

"Do you validate parking?"

"Yes, if that will shut you up."

"Good. I'll be over first thing in the morning. What time do you open?"

"8:30. My paralegal will deal with you. Name's Rafael Sugar. Came to us through Putnam. He's sweet, like his name." This time his cackle sounded more sarcastic than sinister.

So it came to be that I inherited 21 legal-sized yellow tablets, bearing 652 handwritten pages which Geoffrey had titled "Dark Tales of Hollywood and Other Sad Stories." Underneath it, he'd penciled in and crossed out several subtitles: 'An Expert's Exposé of the Fame Game;' 'Tinseltown's Not the Only Place where People get Paid for being Weird;' and 'An Insider's Map of the Potholes on the Treacherous Road to Fame.' Clearly, the adage 'Less Is More,' held little appeal for Geoffrey. But, despite his lurid titles, I determined to plow through his efforts over the upcoming July Fourth weekend, which I'd been invited to spend at a friend's retreat in Palm Desert.

There's something gloriously clichéd about reading a manuscript beside a Southern California swimming pool while endlessly flowing Margaritas and Speedo-clad buttocks fly by. Predictably, the refreshments made evaluating Geoffrey's outrageous hyperbole tolerable. Despite his fondness for tautology and prurient physical description, I found several of his subjects compelling and, by week's end, determined to see if I could make something of his sprawling opus, hardly anticipating the Herculean task awaiting me.

For the next decade I struggled to distill Geoffrey's tall stories and unholy cast of characters into a credible read. Periodically, I had to give it up as a lost cause and let the worried pages gather dust. Structuring tenses has never been my long suit, nor apparently was it Geoffrey's. He juggled Present Perfect with Past Continuous, then doubled back to Present Continuous and finished with a Future Perfect flourish, *all on one page!* Eventually, with the acquisition of a computer, I could no longer cite the drudgery of retyping as an excuse. Again, I labored to bring some sense to his screed and again I failed.

It was not until I leased a second home in New Orleans' fabled Pontalba Apartments when I realized the exigencies of life and career had done me an invaluable service. The years of struggle, combined with the laissez-faire character of the French Quarter, had worn away my inherent New Jersey prudery—that judgmental force that kept me from transcribing objectively, the stories of those folks Geoffrey Putnam had so long ago called his "BCs."

Emancipated by this apotheosis, I returned to his tablets with renewed determination. Along the way I was emboldened to add a couple BCs of my own, heartened by knowing how much that would surely have pissed off Geoffrey.

With typing THE END came the cognition that, in this life, all the really interesting people are "BCs." Maybe even me and thee, dear reader.

C. Robert Holloway—November, 2009

DeDe Dixie

Geoffrey wrote that his private line would ring every Thursday around 10:00 AM. He always knew it was DeDe before he picked up the receiver and this was long before Caller ID. For nearly four decades, her syndicated column, *DeDe Dixie's Tinseltown* appeared in more than 280 newspapers across North America.

"It's DeDe. I'm stuck for a tag item for this week's column. You're the only one can save my ass. Nothin' too nasty or mean. You know I can't run it if it's nasty or mean—or too sexy. I know my readers—mostly small-town housewives. They don't like smut and they hate anything too spiteful—and they pay my rent."

Geoffrey figured she routinely made this, 'I know my constituency' speech to reassure herself, but lately, there was something odd about her voice. "You got a cold, DeDe?"

"No, I don't have a goddam cold," she snapped, defensively. "It's this fuckin' heat! The pollen count is way up, and Christ knows what kinda' crap is in the air. Whatever it is, it's sure as hell workin' my asthma. I can't hardly breathe," and she coughed violently, as if in further testimony. "Shit, now this goddam phone's goin' dead. Hold on while I find the one in the living room." After some clicking and humming, she asked, "Can you hear me?" to which Geoffrey answered he could—just fine.

"Good! I was hopin' maybe one of your clients was lookin' over those miniature turnips at the Mayfair—that kinda stuff. My readers love items about what kind'a food the stars are eatin'".

"Most of my clients have their groceries delivered, DeDe. I've told you that *how many times* before?"

"Well pardon me, Mr. Fancyass."

"And my guess is that the ones who do their own shopping, don't do it at the Mayfair."

"Or breathe the same air as the rest of us. Forgive me, I forgot." She wheezed painfully. "Maybe that's my problem. I should be breathing some of that Beverly Hills air."

"Or Bel Air," he suggested. "Better air in Bel Air."

"Oh, now that's real cute, Geoff! You and your word play. You might want to copyright that one—maybe sell it to the Chamber of Commerce."

"Thanks, but I'm fairly sure Bel Air doesn't have a Chamber of Commerce, DeDe. Contradicts the whole point of the place, don't you think?"

"Don't confuse me with facts. I deal with enough of them all day. Which reminds me, I been meanin' to ask you forever, 'cause I know you'll know, if anyone will. What's Travolta's story? Is he or isn't he? I'm askin' you 'cause wasn't one of your clients connected to that crackpot Sciencology for awhile? If they still are, no offense, but what the fuck is that all about? Not that I'd write anything . . ."

"It's Scientology, not Sciencology," Geoffrey corrected her, gently.

"Big difference! Don't stop my train. I was havin' lunch with Ann Miller and Claudette Colbert the other day, and the subject came up. Claudette said 'No way', and Ann said, 'Are you kiddin'? Travolta is queerer than a Chinese typewriter.' So, what's the scoop, Poop? Strictly off the record, of course."

Geoffrey knew this line of questioning was an onramp to hell and could never be answered to her satisfaction. When he first arrived in Hollywood, he'd been advised by an exec at Paramount—to survive a relationship with DeDe Dixie, you'd best anticipate that line of questioning and avoid answering it at all costs. Anecdotal reports would infuriate her, street gossip would make her less so, but anything short of first hand experience—and, *if he had had it,* why would he tell her?—she wouldn't believe anyway.

"How many times are you going to ask me that, DeDe?" he fired back. "I hear the same scuttlebutt you hear. Short of catching Travolta *'en fladickto'* with a video camera, what's the point?" He knew she loved that kind of bluish word play, which usually provoked a hearty laugh. Once again, it did, and got DeDe to change the subject.

He first met Delphinia Dixie (she swore it was her real name) in the subterranean garage shortly after moving into Harper House, two decades ago. A tiny lady with honey-blonde hair that gave her a startling resemblance to Dinah Shore, she was struggling to park her outsized Buick convertible in her undersized stall. The golf bag in the back seat, sprouting an assortment of snooded clubs, convinced him it was Dinah. "Would it help if I guided you, Miss Shore?" he offered.

"No, but if you parked that tank of yours closer to the wall it would make my life a lot easier," she snapped. "And thanks for the nothing compliment. Shore's a helluva lot older than me," she said, arching her neck to flatten the wrinkles. "You gonna' tell me your name or am I supposed to guess it?"

And so began their acquaintance—too flinty for Geoffrey to think of as a full on friendship. DeDe informed him she'd been born and raised in Charleston, that unofficial capital of the genteel, 'hush-mah-white-mouth' South where she graduated from Ashley Hall School for Girls. Despite her white-gloved, Mary Jane-patent-leathered upbringing, DeDe's fondness for emulating the profanities of a San Pedro stevedore offended Geoffrey's affinity for proper speech. He often found himself flinching at the number of times she used the 'F' word in a sentence.

Then again, DeDe could be disarmingly deft at switching topic and tone. This day, her voice seemed more 'bourbon and branch water' than he remembered. Particularly given how many times she bragged about having given up smoking 'a hundred years ago.'

"Honey, did you see "The Cat's Meow"—Bogdanovich's thingie about Hearst and Marion Davies?"

"Yes, and I liked it."

"So did I." She sounded relieved at the prospect of not having to argue. "Ed Hermann's best work!"

"Agreed. Hermann called me about representing him," Geoffrey crowed. "But I had to turn him down. Not enough of a household name." That said, he wondered when the other shoe would drop as there was inevitably a 'gotcha' when DeDe waxed enthusiastic about anyone's talent.

"Too bad there wasn't a goddam word of truth to it." Usually 'Princess of the Pregnant Pause', this time DeDe faltered. "Wanna' know how I know?"

"I'll bite, if you promise there's no worm."

"What the fuck's that supposed to mean?"

"The apple? Adam and Eve? Silly metaphor. Sorry."

"You're forgiven, though I still don't know what in hell you're talking about. You know I started out with Louella Parsons. I was one of her researchers. Lolly—that's what everybody called her—Lolly was very loyal to her staff—didn't pay us for shit, but she was loyal and protective. She called us her 'gofer angels,' which we were."

"This is eventually going to lead back to "The Cat's Meow, right?"

"If you'll shut up for a goddamn minute . . ."

"Sorry," he replied and instinctively placed a hand over his scrotum.

"Christ, now my fax line's ringing. That means they're gettin' antsy in New York. I'll call you right back."

"Alright, but I'm only here for another 20 minutes or so."

"Don't leave 'til I call you back. I need help, remember?"

This was not DeDe's usual pattern, but Geoffrey let it slide and returned to his work—but not for long. She called back in less than five minutes. "The fax was from Saul, my editor. Wants an item about the trend toward Christian Family films. Like I told ya', my readers don't like a lot of smut."

"Too bad, DeDe. Most of my clients wallow in it."

"I'm ignoring that for the smart-assed remark it is. Now, where the fuck was I? Oh, yeah—Lolly's daughter, Harriet Parsons was a dyke, one of the nicer ones—and a film producer—she died a few years ago and her longtime girlfriend, I forget her name—they actually had a marriage ceremony in Vegas, or some goddamn place—anyway the girlfriend is still around, calls and gives me a tidbit once in awhile—*unlike some people I know*. 'Maddie,' that's it! I asked Maddie if she'd seen "The Cat's Meow, and she said she had and liked it, but that Lolly had always maintained to Harriet that she'd never set foot on Hearst's yacht, then alone witnessed a murder on it. I can't imagine why Lolly would lie to her own daughter."

"Why wouldn't she?" Geoffrey countered. "A pact with the devil is a pact with the devil."

"Because she was her own flesh and blood, for Christ's sake! Something you gay men never understand. A parent doesn't lie to their own flesh and blood."

"Tell that to Nixon's daughters."

"Don't get political on me."

"I'm not. But if you think Louella Parson's deal for a lifetime job with Hearst—keeping silent about witnessing the murder of William Ince didn't mean keeping her mouth shut with *everyone,* then you're hopelessly naive."

"Just because everybody in Hollywood passed that rumor around, sure as hell doesn't make it fact," she retorted.

"Isn't this fun?" Geoffrey chuckled. "God knows where we'd be by now if you'd *hated* the movie."

"You're awfully long in the tooth to be a smart ass, Geoff," she said, but the giggle in her voice signaled he'd successfully negotiated yet another Dixie-laid minefield."

"You going to write about it in your column?"

"Maybe. Maybe not. Just trying it out on you."

"Glad to be of service," he quipped. "You owe me."

"In your dreams. So, you got anything I can use, Baby? Something from the Mayfair Market? Anything, for Christ's sake?

"Alright. How's about this. I spotted Angelyne in her pink Camaro convertible around midnight a couple nights ago. She wiggled into the market clutching her pink poodle and a couple of screamers—her hair burners, I'm guessing. She looked a thousand. That creepy, crepey face of hers peeking out between those enormous boobs. Had an urge to throw candy corn at her but Halloween is six months away!"

"Very funny! First off, none of my readers will know who the fuck Angelyne is, and secondly, you know damned well I can't put that kind of crap in my column."

"Okay. How about this: Joan Collins cursed out the valet parker at Chasen's last Saturday?"

"Where'd you hear that?"

"From the valet parker's boyfriend. Seems Collins wanted to drag him home and he wasn't interested. Really pissed her off."

"You're hopeless. I use an item like that and I'd be sued in the morning and job hunting by the afternoon. Maybe that's what you've got in mind?"

"Hardly, DeDe."

"Did you happen to notice what Angelyne was buying at Mayfair?"

"Matter of fact, I did."

"Well? I got a deadline here, remember?"

"A bag of ice, two six packs of Corona, three limes and a bottle of Tequila."

"Jesus, really?"

"Figured she was prepping the boys to give her a facial."

"What? Oh I get it. You're one sick SOB, Geoffrey. Thanks for nothin'."

After that conversation, Geoffrey didn't hear from DeDe for many months which stretched into years. He'd long since moved from Harper House to Doheny Towers, removing the possibility of chance encounters in the garage. Her columns continued to appear with metronomic precision in small-town newspapers across the country. As DeDe no longer bothered to make a courtesy call before she mentioned one of his client's names, he presumed she was lifting her quotes from the major tabloids and rephrasing them in her own saucy, backflip fashion. Occasionally, his clipping service would forward a copy—all fairly innocuous stuff—and the prevailing Hollywood maxim, "I don't care what you write, just spell my name correctly," was happily sustained.

Every so often he got a report that DeDe had been seen at a studio screening, squired by a male companion. When he received word that she'd fallen and broken her hip and was likely to be consigned to a wheelchair, he sent flowers and placed a call to her, but never heard back.

One day, just after lunch, his former client, Rachelle Raven called from the set of *Ellery Queen* to ask if he'd seen her name mentioned in a column called "Tinseltown."

"I have no idea what you're talking about, Rachelle," was his quick reply.

"I have it right here in front of me. In the *Media Town Talk*. You may remember, Media, Pennsylvania is my hometown? The boys at the Bucks County Playhouse box-office mailed it to me. It claims I just had my fifth face lift."

"I don't think our clipping service bothers with *The Town Talk*, Rachelle," he said, trying not to sound patronizing. "What's the name on the column?"

"DeDe Dixie's Tinseltown. Says I had it done in Rio, of all places!" Before he could comment, she added, "Everyone knows *if I had one*, it would be done right here in Beverly Hills. Who the hell is DeDe Dixie, anyway?"

After he'd mollified Rachelle at length, he retrieved the only number he had and called DeDe. "Who is speaking?" she answered after only one ring. The voice was far deeper and more feeble-sounding than he remembered.

"It's Geoffrey Putnam, DeDe. We haven't talked in what? 3 or 4 years? But you've been on my mind lately."

"Tell me again, what is it you do, dear?" Something didn't quite ring true for Geoffrey, but Alzheimer's affects no two people in the same way and if that was what he was hearing, he decided to play along.

"Geoffrey Putnam—the press agent? You used to call me every Thursday, looking for a tag item, I think you called it."

"Ah yes. The handsome Geoffrey. The smart-mouthed one." She giggled throatily. "You were never much help, but it *was fun* bantering with you."

"So, how have you been, DeDe? I haven't seen you at a screening in eons."

"I don't get out as much as I used to, dear. It's my knees. All those years of tennis finally caught up with me."

"Tennis? I thought it was golf?"

"Did I say tennis? I meant golf. And my asthma still grips me like a boa constrictor."

"I'm sorry to hear that, DeDe."

"My nephew moved in with me. He's a big help. Does most of my leg work, thank God. You know, the business has changed so. The studios don't send out the volume of . . . ."

"You never mentioned having a nephew."

"Because I never knew little Danny existed until just a few years ago. Almost like he appeared out of nowhere. He's become my guardian angel."

"I'm happy for you, DeDe. Not to change the subject, but one of the reasons I was calling—I was wondering who gave you that item about Rachelle Raven?"

"What?"

"Something about a facelift in Brazil, I was wondering where . . ."

"I'm surprised at you, Geoff! You know I can't reveal my sources. Or Danny's. I'd say, tell that over-the-hill-whore, she should just be grateful to see her name in print."

"Good lord, DeDe! That doesn't sound like you. What provoked that?"

"Danny is smart as whip! He's cultivated informants in clever places—like hair and make-up people and limo drivers. I'll tell you that much."

"Thank you. I'll pass that along to Rachelle—minus the over-the-hill whore part. Ought to greatly relieve her concerns."

"You're welcome. It might be good for you and Danny to meet. I've a hunch you'd like each other. But the lad is so shy, I wouldn't get my hopes up."

"Doesn't sound shy to me, but if you say so. Have him give me a call. Maybe you'd like a copy of my client list? It's not as long as it used to be. Perhaps we could be of mutual benefit—like in the old days."

"Thank you, dear. Like I said, I wouldn't get my hopes up. Bye bye."

For the next several days, Geoffrey struggled to decipher the disquieting nuances in that conversation. But he couldn't. In the past, when he'd found himself in a similar state of mind, he took satisfaction in sending flowers, 'to melt the glacier' he explained it, so he called David Jones, his favorite florist. While placing the order, he had an inspiration. He instructed the clerk, "Tell David, I want to deliver the arrangement myself. I'll drop by the shop around 4:00 this afternoon to pick it up." Thus providing him an excuse to check out his old Harper House digs and maybe get a glimpse of DeDe's world at the same time.

He had Robbie call to inform her that a delivery from David Jones was on its way and to make sure someone would be home to accept it.

"She said she's not going anywhere," Robbie reported. "What a weird voice. Sounds like Carole Channing imitating Tallulah Bankhead under water."

After parking his car under a tree two buildings away from Harper House—just in case someone might be looking out their window, Geoffrey carefully lifted the magnificent arrangement of purple lilacs and white magnolias from the back seat and climbed the stairway to the main entrance. He quickly found 'DDD' on the building directory and, despite a pang of anxiety for what he was about to attempt, pushed the intercom button for #501.

"Who?" was the terse response.

"Flowers for Miss Dixie," he said, in his best deliveryman voice.

"Oh yes. Would you mind bringing them to the fifth floor? Set them inside the door to 501. It's just to the right of the elevator. I'll leave it open."

"Comin' right up, M'am," he answered, delighting in the silly deception. The buzzer sounded, opening the door to the main lobby. As he was about to push the call button, the elevator door opened and a sweet-faced senior emerged, carrying her miniature bull-dog.

"How beautiful!" she cooed. "Are they for Miss Dixie?"

"Yes, how did you know?"

"Lucky guess. I live one floor below her. But since nobody in the building has seen her for such a long time, we were all getting a bit worried."

"I heard she has a nephew that watches . . ."

"Pshaw! That so-called nephew never talks to anyone. So standoffish! Not a word about how she's doing. But it's really none of my business." She leaned to whisper. "I've said too much already."

"Not at all. I used to live here myself—in #101, the duplex right there off the lobby."

"Of course! I thought you looked familiar. I'm Ginger Alcott in #401. Used to have the "Cooking With Ginger" show on Channel 13."

"I remember," Geoffrey said, fibbing mightily. "Geoffrey Putnam. Old friend of DeDe's. I hope to surprise her with these."

"How dear of you. I wish there was some way you could let us know how she's doing? Once in a blue moon, I run into her nephew in the garage, but he's so rude, he never even says hello. Sometimes I hear him yelling in the middle of the night. Just hope it isn't at Miss Dixie. When you see her, please tell her everyone in the building is asking for her and wishing her well."

"I'll do that," he nodded, half-heartedly.

Stepping into the narrow elevator brought back a flood of memories, especially of the stormy night when the power went out all across West Hollywood, trapping DeDe in the elevator—between floors. He was carrying his dry cleaning up from the garage when he heard her screams. Using a flashlight and a coat hanger, he somehow managed to pry the doors open and pull her to safety without spraining anything or breaking anyone's bones. He vividly recalled DeDe's justifiable hysteria while pledging eternal gratitude to him and vowing to 'move out of this shit hole the first chance I get.' That was a long time ago.

He stepped off at the 5th floor, saw the door to #501 was slightly ajar and rang the bell.

"Just leave them inside my vestibule, please," a voice instructed from deep inside the apartment.

"As you wish, M'am," Geoffrey said in his youngest sounding voice.

"I hope there's a note from the sender?"

"There is, M'am. It's in a sealed envelope." Thinking this was the 'now or never' moment, he asked, "Why don't I bring the arrangement in to you?"

"But I have nothing to give you for a tip. Besides, I look a fright."

"A tip is not necessary," he said, and was hit by a terrible smell—a pungent combination of moth balls, camphor and something so acrid, he couldn't immediately identify it.

"Alright, if you wouldn't mind. I'll have to ask you to keep your voice down. My nephew is asleep in the guest room. He works late hours, helping me gather bits and pieces for my column."

He stumbled on the sill between the hall and living room and nearly dropped the metal vase. Recovering, he entered a space so dark he could barely make out where to step next. The curtains were tightly drawn and the only illumination came from a tiny gooseneck lamp on a table beside the figure in the wheelchair.

"Aren't they lovely," she whispered. "Shove some of those magazines out of the way and put them on the coffee table, if you wouldn't mind?"

Geoffrey endeavored to do as asked and nearly lost control of the vase a second time.

"I hope the incense isn't too overpowering. It's for my asthma. These walls are covered with mold."

'Incense!' he thought. 'More like burnt tires!' As his eyes became accustomed to the gloom, he could see (as only a Hollywood Press Agent would) she was wearing Gloria Swanson's turban from *Sunset Boulevard,* Jackie Kennedy's sunglasses from Onassis' yacht and Shirley Booth's bathrobe from *Come Back Little Sheba.* 'Where's her hair?' he wondered. 'Is it possible she doesn't have any left?'

"Hand me the card, please?" she instructed, "and sit over there—not too close, dear. I catch cold easily." She held the little envelope under the gooseneck. "Ah, David Jones," she exclaimed. "I might have guessed. He always makes such lovely arrangements. Must be a very nice man to work for." Her nails appeared to be bitten to the quick, making it difficult to open the envelope.

Geoffrey wondered where this was headed and if he was being sent-up somehow when it dawned on him: DeDe's Southern accent was missing or had been softened to the point of nonexistence. 'Could losing one's accent be another repercussion of Alzheimer's?'

"Now, where have I put my reading glasses?" she fussed. "You'll have to forgive me but my eyes aren't what they used to be," and handed the envelope to Geoffrey.

"No problem," he replied and opened it to read, "For DeDe Dixie, America's favorite Southern belle, from her long-time admirer, Geoffrey Putnam."

"Geoffrey Putnam? He's the one that called just the other day. He reminded me we hadn't spoken for ages."

'Is it possible DeDe was blind as well? Or had the years altered his looks so drastically?'

"So like Geoffrey. And how thoughtful to send lilacs and magnolias."

He decided to play the game a bit longer. "I have a confession, Miss Dixie. My mother has been reading your column in our hometown paper for years, so when I saw your name on the delivery slip, I called her and told her that I might get to meet you. She said to be sure and tell you what a big fan she is—because you never write anything too nasty or mean or too sexy."

"Really?"

"I believe those were her exact words."

"Nice to hear my style has been universally recognized."

Somewhere in the apartment a door slammed shut with such violence it made the wall of photographs behind DeDe shake and caused her to visibly flinch. Suddenly, a wild-eyed, Mestizo-looking man of 20 or so, burst into the room, wearing an embroidered vest over his bare torso, plaid boxer shorts and snake-skin boots. "You got your fuck!" he screamed. "Now where's my dineros?"

Clearly, DeDe was rattled, but steeled herself to speak in a reproving whisper. "Danny, this is the delivery man from David Jones . . ."

But Mister buzzcut, diamond stud earrings, tattooed cross on hairless chest, was having none of it. "I don't give a flying fuck who this dude is. You probably tryin' to get him to fuck you, too! I want my dineros, Mang. You hear me? I'm into my guy for some serious scratch. He wants his Benjamins and I got 'til tomorrow to deliver 'em. You owe me big time, Mang! I want my frickin' money—and I want it now!"

"Just try to calm down, dear. No point in getting so upset over dirty old money." She turned to Geoffrey. "Danny is obviously having a bad day."

"I went to the ATM and it said you changed the fuckin' PIN on your debit card," Danny snarled. "What the fuck's with that?"

"I didn't hear you leave the house, Danny."

"The name's Marco, you fuckin' silly Queen. I'm Marco and I'll always be Marco and I never was Danny and I never will fuckin' be Danny. You got that, putaña?"

Despite the sunglasses, Geoffrey could see a look of total terror had washed over DeDe's face. "Now don't be foolish," she implored. "You're my nephew and that's all there is to . . . ."

"Nephew, my hairy ass! I hate it when you put me through this. I'm Marco—*you're Danny*—when you're not draggin' it up as DeDe. How much longer you think you can get away with this shit? Huh? Huh? How much longer, faggot?"

"It's the drugs," she wailed to Geoffrey. "He's not himself when he's doing the drugs."

"I know you got some green hiddin' under that fuckin' doo-rag thing." He produced a switchblade from his boot and snapped it open. "You gonna play nice and take it off yourself or do I cut it off? What's it gonna be? Huh? Huh?"

DeDe sprang from the chair with startling agility. "Danny, I'm asking you to please put that knife away. There's no reason for you to . . ."

Geoffrey looked for a moment to jump into the fray but couldn't find one. Obviously deranged, there was no stopping the young man. When he yanked DeDe's turban from her head, her sun glasses came with it along with a cascade of $100 dollar bills fluttering to the floor.

"I knew it, *puta loco*! I knew it!" He raised the knife and lunged toward DeDe.

Right out of a Barbara Stanwyck movie, Ginger Alcott appeared in the archway, holding a Beretta 92F and fired off a round just missing Marco/Danny's left knee. "Drop it right there, Beaner!" she commanded. "I may look like just another old lady with a pistol but I've been practicing down at the Gun Club on 6th Street for years. So don't fuck with me!"

"Another *puto loco,*" Marco shouted, as he rushed toward her. "The building is filled with crazy bitches."

Ginger fired a second round directly into his heart, which sent him reeling backwards and blood splattering all around. "Don't say I didn't warn you, Zapata."

DeDe scrambled to put her turban and sunglasses back on, then fell on Marco's limp body, wailing and sobbing. "I think he's dead. My nephew is dead. Somebody do something!" But it was too late. DeDe's Adam's apple had spoken volumes—at least to Geoffrey.

"When I heard all the shouting, I figured it wasn't about those pretty flowers," Ginger explained, "So I called 9/11 and loaded my trusty Beretta."

"We are certainly grateful," Geoffrey declared, mesmerized by what he'd just witnessed and fascinated as to what turn it would take next.

"The Sheriff should be along any minute," Ginger winked at him. "They always bring an ambulance. By the way, have you noticed that awful smell?" she whispered.

"Dede said it was incense for her asthma."

"Incense? Smells like uncooked durian to me." She put the safety on her pistol, placed it in her smock pocket and leaned to console DeDe. "Good gracious, it looks like you're bleeding, dear. There's a cut on your . . . wait a minute! You're not her! Not at all! Not even close! You're Danny—that so-called nephew of hers!" She looked at Geoffrey, imploringly. "Then, where is Miss Dixie?"

On arrival in the basement garage, Hitchcock, the Sheriff's prized cadaver-sniffing dog couldn't wait for the elevator, raced up six flights of stairs, bounded into apartment #501, ran to the back office/bedroom and came to a sniffing halt at the bottom drawer of a file cabinet marked 8 X 10 Glossies—'N through Z.' When Officer Tippi, Hitchcock's handler, tried to slide it open, she discovered it was locked but Hitchcock immediately led her to its key, hiding amongst the paper-clips in a catch-all drawer in the roll-top desk. No one was particularly surprised when they found DeDe's badly decomposed body wedged into the file drawer. She had been neatly folded inside a garment bag.

Several newspapers around the country gave the story bottom of the fold coverage but the California papers went bonkers over it. One upscale handout—and they know who they are—went so far as to publish a glossy, four color, special commemorative edition, complete with a replication of Hitchcock's paw-print on the outside of the notorious filing cabinet.

The weekly tabloids went even further, having made special arrangements with Danny Dixie's (sic) bail-bondsman for permission to take stop-action photographs of him putting on full drag and applying DeDe Dixie makeup in preparation for his first day in Criminal Court.

We'll have to take as final word, Geoffrey's scribbled note at the end of his accounting: 'As Estelle Winwood used to say after a bad rubber of bridge, "We're well out of that, Tallulah."

Geoffrey's Unsuccessful Pitch

"We're well out of that, Tallulah!" he wrote, but apparently Geoffrey wasn't, for I came across carbons of an undated 'letter of inquiry' and sample pages he'd sent to Random House. The response from Bennett Cerf, remarkably short in its shrift, is too devastating to reproduce here. Besides the ubiquitous advice that he should stick to his day job, Cerf called into question whether Putnam was even qualified for that work—"if it any way involves stringing words together in a literate fashion." Small wonder that Geoffrey never made another stab at getting published.

Extract/Sample
"THE TINSELTOWN DRAG MURDERS"
By Geoffrey Putnam, AGOPA*

For nearly four decades, Delphine Dixie's syndicated column appeared in more than 280 North American and Canadian newspapers, without her readers ever knowing who was actually 'telling all' in those titillating panels. The eighty-something's weekly column, 'DeDe Dixie's Tinseltown" was, for its final decade, entirely ghostwritten by an androgynous middle-aged man who, for years, had successfully portrayed himself as Ms. Dixie's devoted acolyte, leg man and long-lost nephew.

Daniel D. Dixie, as he successfully petitioned the California courts to rename himself, entered this life at Mays Landing, New Jersey, baptized as Herman Jeremiah Bradway, the second and least-wanted son of Rev. Joshua T. Bradway, a threadbare but respected Presbyterian minister and his wife, Winifred, both greatly admired by their congregation for being consistently, devoutly colorless.

To understand the Reverend's lifelong loathing for his second son, one needs only to know that Winifred was called to her heavenly rest just two days after giving birth to her yet-to-be-named boy. Since she and the Reverend had been practicing abstinence for over a year, Winifred was hard-pressed to explain to anyone, herself included, how she'd ever become pregnant. As there was no one except Joshua with whom she would dare exchange possible theories, and he had categorically refused to allow any word on the subject, it was later concluded by the Ladies Altar Guild that Winifred had died of embarrassment.

As for the Reverend Bradway, despite his life-long prayers on the subject, it was to his profound shame that he never succeeded in erasing the anger in his heart directed at Herman for causing the irreversible diminution of his career in the service of the Lord.

For half a century, during the spring and summer months, the Mays Landing Lakeside Amusement Park was destination for a thousand Protestant Church outings. From Junior High on, Herman had been forced to work at its Bumper-Car and Roller-Rink Pavilions, always subservient to Charles 'Chuckie,' Bradway, his loutish but favored older brother. Ergo, Herman could hardly wait for the time when he could escape and on a sweltering afternoon in mid-June, the day after graduating from Oak Crest High, where he was scholastically rated as number 46 in a class of 48, he did.

His first stop was Philadelphia, where he found immediate work at a Cheese Steak stand, slicing baguettes and frying onions on the midnight-to-eight shift. He was let go after a month on suspicion of pocketing tips that were meant to be split among the higher-ranking steak fryers.

Next stop, Chicago where he served as towel boy and back-up masseur at the Division Street Turkish Baths. Late one night, a low-level but big-tipping gangster-type complained to the manager that for $20. he expected full release but Herman, despite charging extra for donning rubber gloves, hadn't made the slightest effort to bring him anywhere close to that state. The manager had no choice but to bid, 'Adios' to Herman, so on his way out the door, he hustled an Andrew Jackson from the older, less demanding patron everyone referred to as Judge Daley, and boarded the Greyhound for Denver.

There he landed the job of beheading, skinning and marinating rattlesnakes, a time-honored delicacy served at The Buckhorn Exchange, the city's oldest restaurant. As is often the case in populist cuisine, Herman's total lack of preparation for this specialty worked in his favor. Knowing absolutely nothing about anything culinary gave him a fearlessness over the blending of herbs and spices, emboldening him to substitute California muscatel and horseradish for the traditional Seagram's Seven and Worcestershire sauce. Soon, long time-time Exchange patrons were raving to management that their rattlesnake appetizer had never tasted better! And, while they had such a genius working in their marinating crypt, they might want to be thinking about canning and marketing it under the Buckhorn label. One old-timer, a retired silver-miner, vowed to treat his entire family to the provincial delicacy. "Especially my great grandkids," he declared. "They need to give up that goal-danged KFC and try some real food."

Surprisingly, it wasn't the imminent danger of the work that forced Herman to give up on the mile-high city, but its altitude, which brought migraine headaches and violent nosebleeds on him, maladies nearly impossible to cope with while reaching into a barrel-full of disoriented rattlers.

Next stop, San Francisco, where a series of disastrous one-night stands in the Castro led him to a night-course in Sexual Surrogacy at USF. Unfortunately, all but one of his fellow students, a closeted lesbian dominatrix, found Herman so unattractive, he wasn't able to complete the required homework. And, to make things worse, out in the field, he couldn't even give it away!

Discouraged but not quite suicidal, he flirted with the Hare Krishna for a few weeks after tasting their Chickpea Subji. On learning it was free, he declared their Sambar and Brown Rice was the best he'd ever tasted and bared his chest to all but a hibiscus lei, donned a turban and saffron pantaloons and volunteered to sell the sect's "God Is Elephant" pamphlets in the Dodger Stadium parking lot.

Within minutes, the Security Guards asked to see his permit, and when he couldn't produce one, politely asked him to leave. Herman refused, defiantly calling them 'religious bigots and Nazi Pigs' which forced the younger, less tolerant of the two Guards to pull the safety pin on her Pepper Canister and point it directly at him. "Move your ass now or I spray you, Honkey Krishna," she warned, meaning it.

"Like I'm supposed to think that's for real?" he taunted her. "Woo-woo, I'm scared, Miss Thing!" he said as he lunged for the weapon.

She had no choice but to let him know it *was* for real, then hauled him off, blinded, sneezing and crying, to the City lockup. After three days, when no one from the Krishnas showed up to post bail, he figured it was the universe's way of saying 'time to move on.'

On release, as an act of contrition, Herman made a gift of the unsold "Elephant" pamphlets to the smiling Albanian manning the newspaper kiosk just outside the jail, and as if his prayers were being answered, even if his Father's weren't, he spotted The Chronicle's front-page story about a bumper harvest being reported across the state.

Hoping to find comfort in 'real' labor, Herman worked his way down the California coast picking artichokes at Castroville, avocados at Fallbrook, garlic at Gilroy; he shook nuts from the Macadamia bushes encircling Santa Barbara and graded and packed strawberries from the fields at Oxnard. This back-breaking but honest labor provided him with valuable time for reflection and a semi-attractive, uneven tan. It also helped him shed a few pounds and save a couple hundred dollars.

If one listened closely, the siren song of Los Angeles could be heard reverberating all the way to Oxnard, and Herman *was* listening closely. And, if one took the Ventura Freeway between 3 and 4 am, Los Angeles was only an hour and a half away. With some calculation and a bit of luck, Herman talked his way onto the tailgate of a pick-up truck filled with crates of hand-culled strawberries destined for the Mayfair Market in West Hollywood.

Within an hour of unloading the luscious cargo he had charmed the store manager into letting him begin work as a bagboy despite being told that Mayfair's policy discouraged the acceptance of tips for helping old ladies load their bags into their cars. "No problem! Service is my middle name," he bragged through his farm-fresh tan. That evening he checked into the Hollywood YMCA and by Saturday morning, could be seen standing on Sunset Boulevard, beneath the Beverly Hills marker, hawking maps to the Stars Homes.

Holding down two jobs seemed the perfect solution while Herman deciphered the lay of the land, since it was evident he would never hold that title himself. Then, one bustling afternoon, DeDe Dixie came into the Mayfair, inquiring about miniature vegetables, and the rest, as they say, is history.

Once conversant with Herman Bradway's painfully checkered past, who would think to deny that the fickle hand of fate must have finally decided to jab her finger in his face that day?

—

Suggested Pre-publication teaser

In "THE TINSELTOWN DRAG MURDERS," noted insider Geoffrey Putnam's highly anticipated exposé, inspired by and reminiscent of "In Cold Blood" and "All The President's Men", will set the record straight on the question of manipulation, revenge, lust, malice, ruthless ambition, spiritual betrayal, financial mayhem, sexual perversion, blackmail and, yes, even the occasional murder that plagues the modern-day movie industry.

By chapter two, the discerning reader will find him or herself appreciating the protracted jail-house negotiations that went into convincing Daniel D. Dixie, née Herman Bradway—this self-made psychopath, to unlock his roman-a-clef-styled diaries and bare his soul. In the end, what won the day was a combination of dogged persistence on the part of investigative public relations scribe Putnam and Bradway/Dixie's concern for his reputation in the pantheon of time-honored motion picture journalists. Those privileged few insiders who have read the galleys for "THE TINSELTOWN DRAG MURDERS" predict it is destined to become 'a real barn-burner.'

*American Guild of Press Agents

Preamble to
Forgive Me Father

It was clear that Geoffrey had enjoyed a good deal of travel abroad, as several of his tablets were laced with detailed marginalia about international destinations and his exploits while visiting them. He was especially fond of London for its theatre, he loved Paris' cafés and discos, Barcelona's Las Ramblas, the museums of Florence and the baroque splendor of Vienna's concert halls. The islands of Myconos and Santorini came in for special mention but it was Rio de Janeiro and its slim, bronzed populace that Geoffrey couldn't seem to say enough good things about.

Shortly before he died, Geoffrey introduced me to the young man featured in the next story. By then, Diogo DeSilva appeared to be in his mid-20's, was playing a Latin heartthrob on *General Hospital* by day and choreographing his own modern-dance company at night. More than a year passed before I read Geoffrey's take on Diogo's story and several months later before I managed to track Diogo down and ask him to confirm or deny its authenticity.

He read through it quickly, laughed a lot, confessed that it was essentially all true and expressed hope that, for his family's sake, it would never be published in Portuguese.

Forgive Me Father

At just 8 ½ years, Diogo DeSilva had arrived at several surprisingly sophisticated questions concerning the mores and manners of the upper-middle class Carioca society into which he'd been born, the most troubling being "What exactly is cardinal sin?"

A lithe, bordering-on-pretty, bronze boy, the DeSilva's fourth and last born came to expect deference as his due from parents, relatives, teachers and playmates in the Aproador neighborhood of Rio de Janeiro.

With his Day-glow orange backpack doubling as bookbag and pedestrian-crossing sign, Diogo could regularly be seen scampering between the DeSilva home, Our Lady of Mercy Escola and Candalária Church, situated along Rua Francisco Otaviano, the district's famous main street. The magnificently baroque Candalária, anchors the southern end of Francisco Otaviano and is ministered by the 50 year-old, highly respected, occasionally feared, youthful-looking, Reverend Father Ignatius.

Diogo's parents, educators both, shared a life-long concern for social issues, were totally committed to the charitable efforts of the Catholic Church and fervently encouraged their sons to become altar boys under the beloved Father Ignatius.

In contrast to his brothers, Mateus and Santos, each of whom had served with distinction, the honor of being an altar boy held no attraction whatsoever for Diogo. Rather, from earliest memory, he preferred to jeté about the family courtyard, imagining it to be a grand municipal stage and himself its premiere danseur. He was sure all that wine pouring, wafer dispensing, candle lighting and vestment handling would only cut into his precious dreamtime—already eroded by stacks of homework, catechism study and having to read from the Bible every afternoon to his near-blind grandmamma, Eugênia.

Add in that Diogo was bored with being regarded as dutiful and angelic. To hear his far less obedient playmate Valentim tell it, he and a few others were having all the fun—periodically suspended from Escola, restricted to their bedrooms for days where they could experiment with all manner of wickedness, unobserved. Oh, how he envied them!

Because of Valentim, recent visits to the confessional had left Diogo feeling humiliated, sure he'd disappointed the priest with his pedestrian sins. "Forgive me Father, for I didn't say 'Thank you' to my parents for the new pair of Nike's they bought me; Forgive me Father, for I wet the bed during a bad dream last Tuesday; Worse, Father, I didn't always say all my required prayers at bed-time."

Diogo was sure he heard Father Ignatius snoring during his last confession. And loudly! So embarrassing. It seemed as if the priest could hardly wait to dismiss Diogo and replace him with someone capable of confessing more imaginative transgressions, sins that required more draconian penance.

'Exactly what was a cardinal sin, anyway?' Diogo wondered. 'And just how bad could its penance be?' Perhaps—just perhaps, confessing to something really nasty would, once and for all, get him out of having to follow in his brothers' footsteps. It was certainly worth a try.

Next afternoon, after reading Grandmamma into deep slumber, he inserted fresh batteries in his Walkman and leaped around the courtyard to the strains of Ravel's *Bolero*, mentally practicing his new, improved confession: "I cursed my Papa behind his back; When Mama wouldn't let me stay overnight at Valentim's, I kicked her in the shins and made her cry; I stole 20,000 cruzeiros from Grandmamma's purse while she was napping. I was going to give the money to the Poor but changed my mind and bought cigarettes and rum for my friends, instead." The idea of actually having done such things made Diogo shiver with pleasure. 'Must be why so many people sin!' he figured.

Still, those acts might not be bad enough for Father Ignatius to banish him from the altar altogether. What else might he confess to? He'd recently overheard Mateus and Santos whispering about a bet they'd made over which one could get his girlfriend to 'suck him' first. But his brothers were regarded as being so devout, it was hard to imagine why getting some girl to suck them would be considered a sin. More likely, it would be a privilege. He'd have to give sucking some more thought. Maybe screw up his courage and ask his brothers to explain exactly why it *was* a sin? 'Course, that would involve admitting he'd eavesdropped on them and that could get tricky.

It was family tradition for the DeSilva children to go to confession on Saturday morning, 'So as to be clean and pure for Sunday Mass,' was the logic. Their parents sought absolution late Saturday afternoons, taking turns wheeling Grandmamma Eugênia to the Candalária, contingent on her bowels being cooperative. Their relative silence always put the entire family in good spirits.

The slogan on the Nike box had been taunting Diogo for some time until, inspired, he resolved to 'Just Do It!' on Saturday next. He would time it out so that his two brothers and their 11 year old sister, Sofia, would go into the confessional first. Then the three could return home, leaving Diogo to deal with whatever special punishments Father Ignatius levied on him. If bad enough, he might be forced to run away from home, rather than face the wrath of his family. Diogo spent the rest of the week steeling himself for the worst.

But, when Saturday arrived, if was obvious God had other plans for how the day was to play out—none of which syncd with Diogo's scheme or the Nike mantra. On the preceeding Wednesday, Santos shattered his collar bone while cheer-leading a UniTech rugby match. This resulted in his being plastered in a body cast and suspended from a scaffolded cot in Hospital Miguel Cuoto. On Thursday afternoon, Mateus complained of stomach cramps and by midnight, had his ruptured appendix removed at Hospital da Lagoa.

Despite every effort to keep this disquieting news from Grandmamma—over the years her blindness had sharpened her hearing to rival a lemur's—she unfairly concluded that her son-in-law's sins, too vile to be mentioned in her pious household, had brought God's vengeance on her beloved grandsons. "For years, I've tried to warn your Mother," she railed at Diogo. "Now, maybe she'll believe me! That imposter posing as your Papa, must go! Divorce is a mortal sin, but annulment is not. I will speak with Father Ignatius about having this terrible marriage annulled, immediately." With offspring ranging from 19 down to 8 ½, Diogo wondered how such an annulment could be accomplished, but knew better than to challenge Grandmamma while in one of her tempers. And nothing he read from the Old or New Testaments seemed to assuage her.

Consequently, on Saturday morning, while his parents raced between hospitals, it was Diogo's unenviable task to escort a fearful Sofia and righteously outraged Eugênia to the Candalária. Once wheeled inside the dank chamber designated for the handicapped, Eugênia let loose with a volley of accusations against her son-in-law that ricocheted off the vaulted stained glass and gilded statuary. The tone of her screeching made Sofia bite her lower lip until it bled and set Diogo's knees to shaking.

For the time being, Diogo thought it prudent not to test the boundaries of cardinal sin and reverted to his old standbys: 'Forgive me Father, for I had another bad dream and wet the bed again. Forgive me Father, but I didn't say all my prayers,' etc. Father Ignatius was snoring before Diogo got to 'all my prayers.' It was hopeless. Flushed with embarrassment, yet determined to get even, he excused himself and silently crept from the confessional.

The following Monday, without informing anyone, he signed up for altar duty. He and three contemporaries began immediate training under Brother Benedito, the hunchbacked monk from Belém whose deformity was so severe, it made his eyes squint. Consequently, he had petitioned the Pope and been given special dispensation to wear dark sunglasses, even inside the church. Diogo thought

Benedito's faux-Armani's looked really cool and hinted for a pair of his own, but was piously ignored.

It wasn't long before Diogo had mastered most of the rituals, and with that, his earlier glow of sanctimony evaporated. As anticipated, he found nothing short of mundane in the lighting and snuffing of candles, the folding and unfolding of sashes and stoles. As for the kneeling, singing and chanting in Latin, what was the big deal? He'd been doing that, albeit from the other side of the railing, all his young life.

Scarcely a fortnight later, with Grandmamma calmed, his brothers' recovery assured by their surgeons and his parents having resumed their heavy University schedules, the Nike slogan, like the serpent in Eden, reared its hissing head once again. Simultaneously, Brother Benedito declared Diogo to be the first of the trainees ready to serve, and handed him a pocket-sized calendar listing the next four Sundays. Diogo's name was penciled in for 8 masses! Of course, confession was mandatory prior to each Sabbath, the first opportunity being but two days away.

All this came as welcome, albeit startling news to Diogo's parents. The question as to why he'd undertaken the training without mentioning a word to them went unasked, offset by their euphoria at such a reassuring turnabout, especially after the trauma and expense of the past weeks. For the time being, all aural evidence of Grandmamma's dyspepsia seemed to be silenced and a renewed pride-in-faith permeated Casa DeSilva.

Instinctively, everyone held their collective breaths, praying it would last.

After saying all his prayers, Diogo went to bed early Friday evening, hoping for a good night's sleep in preparation for the stressful events that lie ahead. Instead, he found himself tossing and turning and broke out in a cold sweat. At midnight, finding silence all about the house, he grabbed his Walkman and earbuds and crept down to the courtyard, eerily lighted by a full moon. Valentim had recently gifted him with a Victoria de Los Angeles CD, which Diogo was sure his friend had stolen, but nevertheless, he commenced miming to the sinuous strains of *Ave Maria*. By 12:30, he'd exorcised his way from tears of exultation to an ecstasy of remorse and back again. Now bored, he remembered Sofia had loaned him her Ricky Martin CD and switched to the sensuous throbbings of *La Vida Loca*. By 1:00 am, having piroretted himself into a near-hypnotic state, Diogo fully anticipated an appearance by the Virgin Mary. And, if the Holy Mother didn't show up, surely Ricky Martin would!

Saturday morning, just after sunup, Mercedes, the family's sturdy housekeeper, stumbled over Diogo's body on her way to the laundry room. After ascertaining he was uninjured and simply sound asleep, she slung him over her shoulder, carried him back to his bed and gently tucked him in. Later, when Mercedes was asked to recount the story, Diogo was unable to recall anything about that fateful night.

One of the percs for an about-to-be confirmed altar boy includes the choice of going to confession alone. By 10:00 am on Saturday, Diogo had decided it was now or never to test the waters—be they holy or not so and he fairly sprinted to the Candalária. First making sure no one was within earshot, he fell into the booth, yanked the door closed, and without preamble, blurted out, "Bless me Father, for I have sinned, I cursed my Papa, I called him a Son-of-a-bitch behind his back."

"Good morning, my Son. Cursing your Papa requires five Hail Marys."

"Thank you, Father. When Mama wouldn't let me stay over at Valentim's, I kicked her in the shins."

"Kicked your Mama? That'll cost you ten Our Fathers and three stations of the cross."

" . . . and made her cry."

"That'll be three more stations."

"Thank you Father. I stole 20,000 cruzeiros from Granmamma's purse while she was napping. I was going to put some of it into the Poor Box, but changed my mind and bought rum and cigarettes for my friends, instead."

The mention of cruzeiros seemed to rouse Father Ignatius. "Is any of the money left?"

"Forgive me, Father. No."

"Well, then—stealing from your sainted Grandmamma is serious business, but withholding money from the church is much more so. Bordering on cardinal sin."

Diogo looked down at his Nikes and felt newly empowered. "I haven't finished, Father. There's more."

"I hope for everyone's sake, your sins don't concern cruzeiros."

"I sucked my older brother's pee pee and then let him stick it in me. It hurt at first, but I began to like it."

"I see. And how old are you, my Son?"

"Eight and a half. I'll be nine in December."

"Which of your brothers made you do this?"

Diogo wavered for a moment. He hadn't thought this fabrication through and was unsure which to name. Finally, certain Mateus and Santos would be on the mend for some time, receiving sympathy rather than interrogation, he blurted out, "Both of them."

Father Ignatius gasped. "I never had the slightest indication they . . ." he muttered, then whispered aloud, "In all my years in the priesthood, I have never heard so many sins confessed by one so young. As God's servant, I'm compelled to look deep into your soul."

With that, he unlatched the perforated screen that separated them, and pulled it toward him. It creaked ominously, indicating it hadn't been opened in a very long time. "I must have Brother Albino oil these hinges," he growled.

"I think you mean Brother Benedito, Father."

"Whatever. Lean close my boy. Let me look upon thy wicked face." Father Ignatius fumbled for his pence nez, which, in his role as confessor, he seldom had need. Once poised on his aquiline nose, the Antinous-like beauty of Diogo came into vivid focus, provoking a gasp of astonishment from the studious man-of-the-cloth. He ran his fingers across the boy's face, stroked his hair, eyes and ears and gently pulled Diogo's mouth close to his. "God may be testing us with a devil bearing an angel's face," he murmured as he pursed to kiss him.

Having seen it performed several times in American movies, and still under the spell of the Nike serpent, Diogo pressed his lips against the priest's and fluttered his tongue deep into the the startled man's mouth.

To say the effect was disorienting would be the understatement of the decade. The words 'indescribably beautiful, other-worldly and rapturously spiritual' leapt about the priest's conscience and brought him to a near swoon. For Diogo, it was more fun than he'd anticipated—the priest tasted like *rapadura,* his favorite candy and, because it was so pleasurable, figured kissing would never be a part of his penance.

Father Ignatius clasped Diogo's head in both his hands. "I have failed God miserably,' he murmured and resumed kissing him all over his face.

Abruptly, a sharp rapping sounded against the mahogany paneling. "Is everything alright, Father?" It was Brother Benedito speaking in an urgent tone. "It's awfully quiet in there. Do you need any help?"

Father Ignatius placed two fingers over Diogo's mouth. Then, smooth as the starched linen of his surplice, he answered. "Everything's fine, Brother Albino. However, when we're finished with our confession, I want you to put some oil on these hinges."

"As you wish, Father," Benedito responded, unable to hide the suspicion in his voice.

"And make sure it's holy oil, Brother Albino."

"My name is Benedito, Father," he answered, petulantly.

"So I've been reminded. Wait in the vestry until I call you." He tilted his head so as to confirm it was Benedito's sandals shuffling away along the terrazzo floor.

"The good thing is those dark sunglasses render him practically blind, the bad thing is they make him suspicious of everything," Ignatius explained. "If this keeps up, I'll have to speak to the Bishop about having him recalled to Belém."

"So, are my sins bad enough to keep me off the altar, Father?

"These walls have ears. Keep your voice down."

"I won't mind, really."

"I don't understand your question."

"Being an Altar boy. Because of my confession, you'll have to cancel my confirmation, right?"

"Not necessarily. Our Lord can be surprisingly forgiving—if we approach him with reverence and play our cards right. That's my job."

"What should I tell my parents?"

"Nothing!" The alarm in Father Ignatius' voice was palpable. "No need to tell them anything! Your 'sacrament of reconciliation' which is the Holy Church's formal name for confession, is strictly between you and your priest. Acts of contrition should never be shared with anyone else. Never! Is that clear?"

"God won't mind me being and altar boy, even if I sucked my brothers' peepees?"

"God tests his children in mysterious ways."

" . . . And then let them stick it in me?"

Before he could make sense of them, the words had escaped the priest's mouth. "On the one hand, you and I have just failed God's little test. On the other, he's given us something to atone for." He hoped the wide-eyed boy would let the elliptical aphorism slide, but he didn't.

"I have no idea what that means, Father. Could you say it again?"

Feeling cornered, Father Ignatius resorted to the classic adult putdown. "That's because you're too young. Your mind is undisciplined. Your ideas unformed."

"Oh, yeah? What if I told you I didn't really steal cruzerios from my Grandmamma or suck my brothers' peepees?"

"Careful! Recanting confession is a dangerous game and considered a mortal sin by the Vatican, my boy. Neither the Bishop of Brazil, the Holy Father nor God Almighty takes to recantations kindly."

Illuminated by the ambient light streaming down on the confessional, Father Ignatius watched in triumph as Diogo's angelic face mutated from confused to crestfallen.

"I need not remind you that what took place here must never be spoken of to anyone."

"But I was hoping . . ."

"I'm sure we can work something out. Special prayers, devoted service . . ."

" . . . to enroll in the Dance Academy."

"Fewer stations of the cross, less Hail Mary's?"

"That would help."

"A month's supply of rapadura?"

"6 months . . ."

"No. That would make you fat. Perhaps a ride in the white Cadillac?"

"The white Cadillac! Really? Then, maybe it could drop me off at the Dance Academy?"

"All things are possible, once I have your sworn pledge. I'll pray to Our Heavenly Father for his endorsement. He hasn't denied me yet."

"Do I still have to be your altar boy?"

"Yes. And from what I can tell, that will make everyone happy."

"Everyone but me." Diogo thought a moment, then burst into his infectious giggle. "Tell me again, Father," he asked, as he kissed him full on the mouth. "How many Hail Marys you giving me for this?"

Disclaimer
Mary Ann & Percy

Of all Putnam's stories, this one gave me the most difficulty—and not just for its subject matter. Its original length, more than double what appears here, was challenge enough to pare down, but, after reviewing miles of microfiche at the public library, I realized he'd used actual names and addresses. Even more bewildering, I discovered he had kept, for an extended time, a second apartment in that same neighborhood. For a Boyfriend? As a clandestine getaway? We will never know as the neighbors have long-since closed ranks and refused to acknowledge any part of this tale.

Mary Ann & Percy

We'll never know how much effort Mary Ann and Percy Norton exerted so as to blend into their, middle-class, Mid-Wilshire neighborhood. Mary Ann, at 60 something, forced herself to master the basics of cookie baking when she'd much prefer to have Percy pick them up from the little French bakery in Larchmont Village. Percy, having said so-long to 70 some time ago, spent every spare moment reading up on the most effective mulching techniques and how to calculate the precise time to set the sprinklers on their scrupulously maintained front yard.

Mary Ann could be seen most Saturday mornings, delivering her little baskets of goodies to the neighbors, "Enjoy them with the Met broadcast." while Percy, stood curbside, rake in hand, a la Grant Wood's American Gothic, dispensing gardening tips, sought after or not, to any and all passersby.

Both adored having their 75 year-old Tudor-style double townhouse praised and never failed to respond to an inquiry about the year it was built and the name of the architect who had designed it along with several other grand homes in this area,.

"He was a negro. The first. Very famous," they whispered, as if such revelation might provoke racial unrest in this quiet, mixed-ethnic enclave where the Mayor of Los Angeles once lived and, one block over, Frank Lloyd Wright's grandson resided with his second wife and her two teen-aged sons by her first marriage.

That was before things took a catastrophic turn, bringing unspeakable notoriety to the neighborhood. *The National Enquirer* cover story that triggered it, which everyone prayed was nothing more than a pack of lies traded by money-grubbing (read: Greek immigrant) gossips, had, nevertheless, sold a record four million copies!

But all that is cart before the pony. What follows, with minor expurgations to safeguard possible libel, is how Geoffrey set down their story on his legal-sized tablets:

"I'll bet Steven knows how to locate a gas leak, don't you, Steven?"

Before the young man with ash-blonde hair and azure-blue, slightly crossed eyes could answer, Mary Ann rushed on, maintaining her docent's smile, one she'd determined years ago best flattered her decidedly oval face. "Percy is so bad at anything mechanical, aren't you Percy? I can't even get him to tack up a no-vacancy sign on the other half of the house. Afraid he'll smash his thumb or some darned thing, aren't you, Percy?

Certain her brother wouldn't respond, for he rarely did, Mary Ann plunged ahead. "I've been smelling something funny down in the basement for days now. No doubt about it. They say you're supposed to call the Gas Company, but I hate having one of those Puerto Rican Wetbacks they have working for them these days—snooping around our property. 'Casing the joint,' isn't that what they call it?"

Steven shrugged as if he'd never heard the expression before.

"Supposing it's a false alarm?" Mary Ann raced on. "We've exposed ourselves to a potential robbery and for what? Like I said, I keep asking Percy to check it out, but he works such long hours by the time he gets home, he's too worn out to do anything but water the lawn, and sometimes he's too pooped to do even that, aren't you, Percy?"

Her questions seldom required an answer, save an occasional shrug or nod, which, nonetheless, caused excessive strain for Percy. Steven sat between them, nodding in vacant agreement, clutching a copy of the *New Illustrated King James' Bible,* in anticipation of reading a verse or two aloud, which he'd been doing every Wednesday, for several weeks.

The three were gathered in the dining room beside an ersatz Victorian table, piled high with old *Los Angeles Times, Harper's Bazaars, Town and Countrys* and *Southern Living*s, subscribed by Mary Ann, much to Percy's parsimonious consternation. Without fail, *The Los Angeles Times* went unread by either of them, though she was quick to remind Percy that its 5:45 arrival on their front steps every morning provided him with a reliable wake-up thunk and her with visible proof when claiming, on virtually any subject, "I read an article about that in the *Times* just the other day." Their Ecuadorian, Korean, Greek, Filipino and Mexican neighbors seemed genuinely impressed at her demonstrations of literacy. Not so, the two English-speaking families in their fringe-of—Hancock Park neighborhood, who, having long ago suspended all conversation with Mary Ann and Percy, knew better.

In her defense, the toney articles and sexy pictures in the glossy magazines infused Mary Ann with a feeling of zestful hope, one of being au courant with all the latest in fashion and décor, not a trace of which was reflected in her daily life.

Steven, a free-lance house-painter, sat wondering if he was expected to thank Mary Ann for her acknowledgement of his presumed abilities or assure Percy that being mechanically inclined, while one of God's special gifts, wasn't the only one The Almighty had bestowed on him. The more he concentrated on picking the right moment to make his point, the more his eyes seemed to cross and skew his vision, the onset of which Steven was unaware. This condition mostly happened when he was in conversation with older folks whose ideas tended to be complicated. His focus blurred when he intuited their hidden agendas, and, if he suspected they didn't have one, he would panic, thinking he'd missed something and his eyes would cross their worst. A distinct ringing in his ears followed and finally, everything within his view took on a blue refraction and shimmered into a double, sometimes triple image. Steven long ago concluded this must be what the church elders meant by "allowing the holy spirit into your soul."

Just now, he was seeing two Mary Ann Nortons and two Percy Dewitt Nortons, this peculiar brother and sister who'd befriended him so determinedly but a short time ago. From the moment he'd given them an estimate on painting their back porch, they'd taken him under their wing. Steven had found it difficult to focus on either of them, but something kept drawing him back, nevertheless.

Mary Ann paused to check her benign smile in the dust-covered mirror languishing against the wall over the sideboard. Percy had never re-hung it after the last earthquake and she must have asked him a thousand times over the past five years.

Un-hung mirror aside, she couldn't recall a night when she'd looked prettier. Her authentic peasant blouse from Costa Rica, with its gossamer-thin rayon ruffle of machine-stitched eyelets trimmed in orange rick-rack hugged her slender shoulders perfectly. When she stood or moved about, a hint of navel showed below its scalloped hem and above the waistline of her stone-washed, size four, Jordaches, held up by a saffron-colored scarf she'd twisted into a belt. 'Stunning,' she declared to herself. And hadn't the saleswomen at Bullocks Wilshire Junior Sportswear told her as much—assured her she looked barely a day over forty-five in this ensemble? Her real age was strictly "taboo-land," guarded as closely as the real nature of Percy's work at the Lockheed Plant.

"Why don't you finish your decaf, Steven, and then we can all go down to the basement and look for the source of that smell. Percy, don't even think about lighting up that nasty cigarette! It could start an explosion or God knows what, and . . ."

An alarm sounded in Steven's head. "Excuse me, Ma'am, but I think it's disrespectful to take the Lord's name in vain, in the same breath with cigarettes. For that matter, I think it's disrespectful to take the Lord's name in vain anytime!" Steven held up his Illustrated King James, as if to shield himself from further blasphemy. It being the very Bible the Nortons had given him on learning Greyhound had lost his luggage, its gilt-edged spine vividly reinforced his point.

For a nano-second, Mary Ann's vermilion lips turned poutish. She knew pouts exaggerated her features unkindly, and quickly resumed her "who me?" smile.

"Absolutely, Steven! I can't imagine what came over me. You can ask Percy how strict I am about such things, aren't I, Percy? I was brought up by a devout Christian mother who always said exactly what you just said. 'There's never any need to take the Lord's name in vain." Afraid she was sounding a bit shrill, Mary Ann cleared her throat and continued. "There is never any need whatsoever to voice the Lord's name in anything but praise. I hope you can find it in your heart to forgive me, Steven?"

"Mine is not to forgive, but the Lord God does, I'm sure. Hallelujah and Amen," Steven yelped and kissed the bible. Mary Ann shot Percy her 'do the right thing' look and together, they seconded Steven's 'Amen.'

"Now Percy, if you can find the light switch, we'll go downstairs. I'll just turn off a few of these lamps and be right along. No point in burning every bulb in the house. You two go on ahead. Percy, lead the way. Here's the flashlight. 'Mercy, Percy," she giggled girlishly. I think you'd lose your head if I wasn't around to remind you where you kept it."

She dashed about, turning off the overhead lights in the front hallway and living room. In her mind, there were dozens of chandeliers, torcheres and table lamps blazing throughout the house, but, over the years, Percy's economies extinguished all but the absolute essential ceiling fixtures which cast the harshest, most unflattering light on everything beneath them. Only a young, unlined countenance could survive the glare of those bare bulbs, and it wasn't often anyone with those qualifications visited the Nortons.

Steven, the exception, had fallen into their hands via the former tenants, two gay men who used to occupy the other half of the duplex. Steven had been hired by them to paint the interior of their side of the house just before they moved in. Their choice of wall colors included *Nouvelle Taupe* and *Angel Blush,* and when reported to Mary Ann, had caused her eyebrows to reach for her scalp line. Certain she had rescued Steven from their perverted clutches, she never missed an opportunity to remind him of her heroic efforts.

And, if Steven's version of the story was to be believed, the rescue came none too soon. In an emotional outburst that even Mary Ann found melodramatic, he'd reported how his innocent offer to rub the older homosexual's back had turned into near sodomy. A shudder came over Mary

Ann every time she imagined the idea of those two perverts looking at Steven, then alone touching him.

Now, nearly a year after the two fairies (what else to call them? 'Queens' sounded somehow like a compliment, 'Queers' was what they called each other and 'Fags' also meant cigarettes) had vacated the premises, she and Percy had coerced this sweet young man away from all possible carnal temptations, all opportunity to mix with his contemporaries, and drawn him into a surrogate family relationship. (He'd once revealed that he was an orphan who'd been adopted by an elderly couple in Seacaucus, New Jersey with whom he'd subsequently lost all contact and he guessed himself to be about twenty-four years old.)

A pleasurable shudder engulfed Mary Ann as she descended into the small but remarkably tidy basement, chattering all the while. First, glancing over her shoulder, she closed the door behind her and slid the concealed deadbolt into place. "I'm pretty sure the smell is coming from over in the corner," she whispered, lightly pushing Steven in that direction.

Then, with the precision of a surgical assistant, she grabbed his right hand and held it up while Percy slipped a pair of handcuffs over his wrist. They'd rehearsed this maneuver for months—practiced with a dummy Percy brought home from the First Aid room at Lockheed.

"Nothing to be alarmed about, Steven," she assured him. "You know you can trust Percy and me. We're very fond of you."

Mildly confused, Steven asked, "What are you doing?" and his eyes began to cross. Percy slipped a second pair of cuffs over his left wrist, the other half of which was clamped around a galvanized pipe spanning the massive wooden beams overhead. Two more sets of ankle chains, their ends bolted to the cement floor, were used to secure Steven's legs. He commenced to see in triplicate.

Mary Ann stared at him lovingly. "We're not here to hurt you. We're here to help you expand your love for Christ—by reliving his time on the cross. Isn't that right, Percy?"

Percy, adrift in tumescent anticipation, managed a lugubrious, "Whatever you say, Mary . . . Magdalene."

For Steven, the ratcheting sound of the hand-cuffs foretold a terrible finality.

"Relax, my darling. We're not so crude as to drive nails through your hands or feet. We think that would be carrying things a bit too far, don't we Percy?"

Percy shrugged, indicating exertion and anticipation was taking a rapid toll. "Thank you, Judas," Mary Ann replied, as if he'd actually said something.

"Steven, from now on you will address me as Mary Magdalene and Percy as Judas, do you understand? It's even nicer if you call him 'my beloved Judas.' We'll address you as Jesus Christ, our very own savior."

Steven's eyes were hopelessly crossed. Somewhere in his head the sound of a double-barreled shotgun exploded with deafening repetition. Blinking back tears, he pleaded, "You're just kidding with me, right? Tell me you're just kidding with me? It's okay if there's no real gas leak, but these handcuffs hurt and I don't get the joke."

"This will help, dear Christ." She unscrewed a bottle of amyl nitrite and jammed it under his nose, dribbling some of the stinging liquid onto his lower lip. "Just breathe in deep. Make you feel a lot better—get you past these first anxious moments."

Steven tried to avert his head, but MaryAnn kept the brown bottle snugged against his nostrils. "Don't force me to pour it down your nose, sweet Jesus, just breathe in slowly." The residual fumes were having an effect and she began to slur. "Judash is going to prepare you for your ascension now, aren't you, Pershy—ah, Judash? Start by pulling off his pants, brother. You always like this part, don't you? Can't fool me. I see that look in your eyes. Pull them off slowly so Jesus can take his own pleasure in the moment. When someone is about to be crucified, they like to do it naked. Says so right there in the New Testament. Need some help, Judash?" she added, reviving her docent's smile.

"You know damn well I don't, Mary Magdalene," Percy hissed, at once thrilled and embarrassed by the prospect. After so many years of unguents, ointments, salves and porno magazines had failed to produce the slightest twitch, this was surely God's hand at work. And, if true, all the planning, practice runs and suffering of Mary Ann's taunts and jeers will have been worth it. Slowly, he pulled the white cotton coveralls down Steven's legs, then, as if nothing could be more natural, crimped them neatly around the young man's ankles.

Taking a pair of garden shears, he cut off Steven's T-shirt and arranged the pieces neatly on the workbench. Steven struggled to focus on something—anything. The whitewashed walls, his manacled state and the amyl fumes compounded his blurred vision and forced him to the brink of nausea. He wished he hadn't gulped down his last supper so quickly—a double cheeseburger, large coke and fries from Burger King. If he could hold on long enough, his captors would explain that this was a Halloween joke, or that he'd somehow missed out on being informed about this form of worship at all those prayer meetings he'd attended since leaving the Navy two years ago. If he could just focus, just stop retching. How was he supposed to put his shirt back together? If he couldn't, where would he find another T-shirt with the logo of the Young Baptist Ministry of Redondo Beach?

"Our sweet Jesus has a very firm body, doesn't he, Judas? Cut off those nasty shorts and we'll see whether or not we'll have to cover him with a loincloth. We love to worship them uncovered, even in this time of great sadness, don't we, Judas?"

Percy managed a grunting assent and with two neat clips of the shears, removed the offending Jockeys.

"Well now, that's not bad, not bad at all," Mary Ann sighed, staring at Steven's uncircumcised manhood, which caused Steven to blush even more, for, of course, he was seeing two appendages.

"Don't you worry, Jesus. It usually happens this way. Nothing to be embarrassed about there. It's your love of mankind showing itself in the form mankind can best understand."

Steven struggled to pull away from her freshly lipsticked mouth, but was so firmly manacled he could only move an inch or two. Overcome with revulsion, he screamed out,

"What are you doing? Why are you doing this to me? I can't believe you're actually . . . ," and began to sob.

Mary Ann withdrew her lips and licked them noisily. "Judas, hand me the crown of thorns. Don't worry, Jesus. This crown isn't as scratchy as the real thing was. We tried the real thing once but it made too many cuts and gouges, so we made this one out of a bread basket. Looks real but without the bothersome after effects." She jammed it onto the young painter's head, causing him to shriek in pain.

"Why me, why are you doing this to me? You are crazy, both of you are crazy. Look, if you'll stop right now, I won't tell anyone anything, I promise. Just stop right now, please? Let me down and we can all pray together and pass it off as some kind of joke. No hard feelings, I promise. Please?"

"No way, Jesus," Percy spoke up. "Once Mary and I have made up our minds, picked a savior to our liking, there's no turning back. You can't appreciate our form of worship unless you experience all of it."

Mary Ann reached for a Polaroid camera and momentarily blinded all three of them with its flash. The photo revealed Percy's formidable gender pressed against his trousers. Elated, Mary Ann goaded him on. "Look what we have here! We haven't seen that Sword of Damocles for a long time, have we, Judas? Bring it out. Give the monster some air," she cackled. "Can't worship the Son of God with a bound-up pecker."

"Dear God in heaven, help me," Steven cried out. "Let us pray, please? Mary Ann? Percy, please let us pray? Almighty God in heaven, please forgive us our sins for . . ."

"Apparently you're not hearing clearly, Jesus. This is Mary Magdalene speaking and this is my friend Judas Iscariot. We'll decide when to pray and when not to," Mary Ann snarled at Steven with a violence not heard before. "We expect you to play the martyr to the best of your ability but don't think you can alter any part of this ceremony, or, and this is really important, implore your Father to help you do it. We are carrying out His very own wishes. He has appeared to us many times in the past, right here in our own home, sometimes down here in the basement and given us special instructions how to best carry out his demands."

His trousers puddled around his heels, Percy stood by awaiting Mary Ann's next move. His knotted brow indicated he was not as committed to the invincibility of God's demands as he was to trying out his rejuvenated weapon.

Mary Ann closed her eyes, rolled her head and commenced to moan in a low-decibel chant, while clutching her breasts through her peasant blouse. "Jesus, I love thee, I have always loved thee and I am destined to bear the son of the Son of God. The way it should have been—the part they always leave out in the Bible. It's not too late. You will command my breasts to fill up. And they will! You'll see." In one convulsive jerk, she yanked the blouse down to her waist revealing two forlorn looking moles. Then, in another voice, one that could as easily deliver a commentary at a fashion luncheon, she added, "Truly stylish women never have big breasts. I've always been a stylish woman and so was Mary Magdalene. They say she was a whore, but I know better. She was a stylish woman who loved Jesus, and because he didn't love her back, she slept around a little, that's all. So they called her a whore. But that doesn't make her one. Not in my book."

She stepped onto the cinder blocks at Seven's feet and wrapped her arms around him. He pulled his head back, choking with revulsion. "No, for God's sake, please, no. Mary Ann, I'm sorry, I mean Mary Magdalene, please let me go." She pressed her lips against his, clenched his tongue between her teeth and bit down hard. Steven shrieked in pain as blood appeared at the corner of his mouth.

"There, there, my sweet Jesus. Mary Magdalene loves you. Loved you then and I love you now and I fear nothing to prove my love to you." She turned to Percy. "The blood looks pretty, don't you think, Judas?"

On a signal from her, he placed an inverted milk carton on the floor directly behind Steven and climbed up on it so as to position himself directly in line with Steven's posterior. Steven writhed about, pulling at the manacles, causing his skin to break and blood to rivulet from his wrists and ankles. Percy dipped his fingers in an open container on the workbench and brought forth a foul-smelling lubricant.

Steven, to his astonishment, though shackled to a water pipe with a cackling, wizened woman wrapped around him and her brother preparing to mount him, had become completely tumescent. "Was this the way it was . . . ?" he wondered, as he drifted toward a faint.

Oblivious to Steven's state of mind, Mary Ann untied the saffron scarf, shoved her Jordaches and bikini briefs to her knees then reached around and grabbed Percy while he, in turn, reached around Steven and grabbed her breasts between his thumb and forefingers. "Are you ready, Judas?"

"I'm ready, Mary." Together they moaned in chorus, "Sweet Jesus, we love you—we love you with all our hearts." Mary Ann took in Steven in one shuddering thrust as Percy pushed inside him with a searing, convulsive lunge. Steven's agonizing screams faded as he neared a complete blackout.

So intent on their individual pleasures, neither Mary Ann nor Percy noticed Steven's head bobbing about lifelessly as they rapidly approached le petite morte. In such close proximity, linked by this young man's body, their 'Jesus of the hour,' it was as if the were united with each other, a sensational thrill that had not gone unnoticed by either of them during previous 'services'.

"Mary, I'm about to deliver my burden to Jesus."

"Our sweet Savior's ready too, if I know anything about it. Go right ahead. We're ready over here, as well."

"Oh, my God. Oh, my sweet Jesus!" Percy moaned and shuddered. Mary Ann commenced to keen and wail, "Mary Magdalene will bring forth the son of the Son of God, after all these years. After all my prayers. At last, I am your beloved. At last, I am your wife." Steven heaved and convulsed, totally beyond control as he surrendered to the shriveled woman impaled on him.

At that precise moment, he regained consciousness and could feel and taste the salty tears coruscating his cheeks. The juxtaposition of sexual sensation and utter despair, mixed with searing physical pain transmogrified him. From some primal and inner place, he began to gurgle and then to giggle and then to laugh aloud. Either he was going mad, or he was the Son of God, or he was the mad Son of God. He was no longer Steven Kirks, house painter, former U.S. Navy ensign and born-again Christian from Lodi, New Jersey.

And such a transforming experience could never have happened to that unworthy creature in the first place. This 'Service' as Mary Ann and Percy insisted on calling it, could only have been endured by a truly holy person. Therefore he just might be that holy person.

Despite his agonizing situation, his debased and painful position, Steven found himself smiling at Mary Ann and Percy, both nodding restfully on his shoulders. He looked heavenward, quietly beseeching God.

"No need to forgive them, Father, for they must know what they are doing."

Redemption?

Follow the instructions:

1) Relax and concentrate on the 4 small dots in the middle of the picture for about 30-40 secs.
2) Then, take a look at a wall near you (any smooth, single colored surface).
3) You will see a circle of light developing.
4) Start blinking your eyes a couple of times and you will see a figure emerging . . .
5) What do you see? Moreover, who do you see?

Apparently a home-devised Act Of Contrition
(found amongst Geoffrey's papers)

Exorcizing the Pontalbas

Since my first visit as a PFC on a weekend pass from the Army base in Ft. McClellan, Alabama, New Orleans has forever held allure for me. The Crescent City, especially its fabled French Quarter, pulsates with mystery, magic and old-world elegance, simultaneously writhing in tawdry excess, unabashed eroticism, and Byzantine, often ludicrous political intrigue—all in welcome contrast to my uptight hometown.

Two and a half decades ago, I determined to live there, while maintaining, for employment purposes, my residence in West Hollywood, CA. To that end, I put my name on the Louisiana State Museum's waiting list for a flat in the legendary Pontalba buildings, which claim to be the oldest in America, having looked down on Jackson Square and the east/west arc of the majestic Mississippi since 1849.

After five years, my patience was rewarded with a lease on a 2nd floor apartment boasting 13 foot ceilings, cypress planked floors, three working fireplaces, nine tall windows opening onto a corner balcony 90 feet long by 8 feet deep, (called a 'gallery' in native parlance) with a breathtaking view of the square and river. The Café du Monde, situated directly across Decatur Street, made it possible to inhale the bracing aroma of chicory coffee and fresh beignets 24 hours a day.

During the first year, between film projects, I furnished its four large rooms with an eclectic mix of American Empire, Caribbean Plantation, Louis XVI, Art Deco, Bombay Company antebellum repros and Ikea proletariat. In an effort to ingratiate myself to the city's movers and shakers, I hosted a series of cocktail parties, dinner parties and holiday events with formal sit-downs for 10 guests, cocktails for 30 and caroling parties for 150. I had it quickly confirmed that, despite daunting parking issues, the promise of free booze and food would lure just about any New Orleanian through the front door and up the staircase.

It was during the second year when the uninvited began to appear—never after an evening of serious drinking, as one would expect, but usually in the early morning, while watering the plants on the gallery, or in the late afternoon, just as I'd begun siesta. My first 7:00 am visitor, a stern-faced female with jet-black hair pulled into a tight bun, floated through my dining room window, buoyed by an enormous hoop skirt. Before she raised her gloved hand and opened her mouth, I sensed she was unhappy about something.

"C'est ce que arrive quand les propriétaires désespèrent de touver des locataires," she sighed. Realizing I had no idea what she was saying, she sighed again and translated. "This is what results when landlords become desperate for tenants."

"I beg your pardon, Madam, but who are you and how did you get up here?"

She ignored me entirely. "Vous n'avez guère le caliber . . . oh, never mind. You are hardly the caliber of tenant we had envisioned in 1851."

I gestured to her costume. "Lady—I don't know what you're going as, but Mardi Gras is several months away!"

" . . . when P. T. Barnum convinced us to install Jenny Lind, the Swedish Nightingale, to promote our new multi-purpose buildings . . ."

I interrupted, cool as I could muster, given the circumstances. "So, I guess that makes you the . . ."

"Exactement!" she snapped, not bothering to conceal her impatience. "Je suis la Baronne Pontalba."

"Of course you are! And I'm James Audubon. Look, lady—I know you have a job to do but my rent check is mailed from my accountant's office in L.A. on the first of every month. Sometimes it takes a bit longer to get here."

"I am not here to collect rent. I leave that Philistine task to my managers."

"Then why *are* you here?"

"My purpose is threefold: First, to review your décor for glaring anachronisms. Secondly, to inform you about some of your illustrious predecessors, and thirdly, if what I see isn't too jarring, point out their secret hiding places."

I turned away, engulfed by an uncontrollable urge to laugh in her face. When I turned back and choked out, "You got my attention with that last bit, Baroness," she had vanished, leaving behind a whiff of sulfur and Violet Musk.

Not ready to swallow the 'Pontalba ghost' legend, I immediately called the Museum office to report the incident, got their answering machine and hung up without leaving a message. Seems it was one of the thirteen legal holidays afforded Louisiana government employees and just as well for I later learned that reports of ghost sightings around Jackson Square inevitably drew yawns from local officials and police alike.

There followed serious misgivings. Had I been too quick to dismiss the woman? Suppose there really were secret hiding places in those 150 year old floors and walls? My imagination kicked into overdrive wondering at the treasures they might contain but I could hardly risk taking a crowbar to the cast-plaster medallions and cypress floorboards.

A few days later, about 4:30 one afternoon, I was drifting off into a much-needed nap when a cackling laugh, not unlike that of the Wicked Witch of the West, made me sit up in alarm.

"Well, jes' look at you, Princess," an androgynous voice shattered my cherished siesta. A shortish male figure, wearing a Panama suit, classic fedora and dark sunglasses stood at the foot of my brass bed.

"Who the fuck are you?" I asked, in my grandest 'intruder-hospitality' tone.

"Gracious, child! Language! We've met before—once on the elevator in mah apartment buildin' in New York and again at Sebastian's on the waterfront at St. Thomas." He jerked his head to one side, looked around the room and cackled again. "I was under-whelmed on both previous occasions and this meetin' looks like it's gonna' sustain the trend."

"I've got to do something about the security around here," I muttered, looking about for anything that might serve as a weapon. "How did you get in?"

"What a silly, inconsequential question!" Oblivious to how his fiendish cackle was working my nerves, he rattled on. "I used to live in the Pontalba, now didn't I? When I was house-sittin' for Beauregard Frampton Plauché, the Third. While Framp was away on his buyin' trips—sometimes weeks at a time—huntin' antiques for his Uptown, blue-haired ladies?" He punctuated every sentence with a question mark and macaw-like cackle. "Beau always hated it when I called him 'Framp,' but I always felt 'Beau' was so commonplace."

"And that bullshit story gives you the right to break in here and wake me up?"

"Trust me, darlin,' your use of vulgarity is not contributin' to your masculine image one iota. Stanley Kowalski you ain't! Now listen up! I'm here to caution you against that ole slut claimin' to be the Baroness Pontalba. She's been workin' that tired act for a century or more. Even tried it on me a couple of times."

A strobe-flash of summer lightening revealed my cackling visitor's face.

"My God, you're Tennessee Williams!"

"Well, Stella by Star! Sleepin' non-beauty has finally awakened. I'd say, let's alert the press, but frankly, mah deah, who'd give a damn? Hee hee!"

"Mr. Williams, I've loved your work ever since I was a teenager and ran away to summer stock and made my professional debut . . ."

" . . . professional debut playin' the newspaper boy in 'Streetcar.' If I had a dollah for every time I heard *that* claim to fame, honey . . ."

"Well, I did, Mr. Williams. I did play him. I was 15 years old at the time, but I can still remember the lines. 'Good evenin', M'am. I'm collectin' for the Evenin' Star . . .'"

"Lord Jesus, spare me. You have any idea how ridiculous that sounds comin' outta your tired ole Yankee mouth? Now, you wanna' learn how to handle the Baroness, or don't ya?"

Unable to stop myself, I added, "Then Blanche says, 'Did anyone ever tell you you look like a Prince out of the Arabian nights?'"

"Christ! Would you stop? I know every goddam line in it! I wrote it, remember?"

"It's just that it was such a big event in my life, Mr. Williams. And I've never had the opportunity to thank you personally. They say there are no small parts, only small actors, but the newspaper boy is an important small part and must be played by a small actor and . . ."

While I struggled to blink back tears of gratitude, he gave me the raspberry, stepped into my free-standing cheval mirror and vanished. There was no resuming a nap after that.

The Williams encounter rattled me much more than the previous one had. Guessing I'd never have a better excuse to forego my thrice-weekly Alanon meetings, I walked around the corner to Tujaques, bellied up to its century-old bar and gestured for the Irish-as-O'Reilly bartender to lean close.

"I heard that Tennessee Williams used to come in here."

"You askin' or tellin', then?" was his cautious response.

I extended my hand. "Hi, I'm C. R. Holloway. Live on St. Ann—in the Lower Pontalba."

He shook it like a surgeon avoiding germs. "The one on the corner—with all the ferns?"

Surprised, I answered proudly, "Yeah, that's me."

"You gotta be more careful when you're hosin' 'em down. Soaked me more than once, I can tell you."

"Sorry about that. That's why I try to water early in the morning."

"Called you a few cherse names, I did."

"Probably deserved them. I promise it won't happen again. So did he?"

"What? Who? Whaddya talkin' about?"

"Tennessee Williams? Did he used to come in here?"

He wiped a glass and held it to the light while surreptitiously checking me out. "Yeah, but you're talkin' years and years ago. Come in here most every time he was in town."

"I want what he used to drink."

"Williams was a martini man. Bombay gin. One olive." I could see the Irishman was warming to the tale. 'Dalt," he'd say, "Just wave the Vermouth cork over the shaker. Then stir it, don't shake it. Bruises the gin."

Despite my antipathy to gin, I said, "Make me one just like Tennessee's. Straight up, if you please, Dalton."

"My pleasure. Might interest ya ta know, Mr. Williams usually smoked a Cuban cigar with his martini."

"Why not? You got one back there?" Having given up cigarettes fifteen years before, I was flirting with real danger, but what the hell!

One martini led to two, two led to three, and just after ordering a fourth, I raced to the men's room in time to wretch everything up, marveling at how the pimento olives managed to remain intact. Tujaques' Peruvian dishwasher was deputized to escort me on the short walk home. I think his name was Cesar, and, though elfin in size, he managed to carry me up the steep, spiraled staircase, hurl me onto my bed, refuse a tip and rush back to work, quietly locking the door behind him. My last thought was, 'Now that I'm this snockered, the apparitions are really going to descend on me,' but I was wrong. I slept dreamlessly for ten uninterrupted hours.

Next afternoon, I dragged myself to my Alanon meeting where my sponsor patiently explained that truly evolved spirits don't like dealing with drunks and rarely visit them. Assuming my first two visitors had long since graduated from the twelve step program, her canon made total sense. She further suggested that I might be better served attending a couple of AA meetings in the big room, next door, but I declined. I had a better idea.

I went directly home and called a few friends. "I'm clearing my bar of all hard-liquor, including brandy, champagne, cordials and liqueurs. Strictly white wine from now on. Come and get it, first come, first served." By 10:30 that night, all but a miniature Cointreau from Delta Airlines had found new homes.

This grand demonstration of will power filled me with pride and a renewed determination to be more open to my spiritual side. My big cognition was this: my home town never had apparitional-type appearances of any magnitude because the place is so boring. New Orleans, on the other hand, with its mystical history richer than any other place in North America, is the perfect convention center for free spirits, errant or otherwise.

I dug out my underused diary and commenced to write when a stout little man, in morning-coat, breeches and silk hose, appeared in my foyer, all but frothing at the mouth.

"Every time I hear the fiacre drivers explain the initials . in the cast iron railings, I want to cut out their tongues," he snarled as he unsheathed his menacing saber. Mercifully, his expansive moustache absorbed most of his spittle. "Jesus Christo!" he railed on, "When will they get it through their stupid heads? A & P stands for Almonaster-Pontalba—not for the grocery store chain!"

"Don't tell me, Mister." I held up the palm of my hand. "You're preaching to the choir."

"Good to know. Gracias, Senor."

"Your name's on the tip of my tongue," I said, quickly adding, "But please don't cut it out! Give me a second . . ."

"Es stupido! My daughter built these buildings with my money—her inheritance.

"I remember. You're Don Andres Almonaster . . ."

" . . . y Roxas ," he added grandly.

" . . . y Roxas.' One of the first 'somethings' appointed by the Spanish crown, right?"

"Royal Standard Bearer. The *first and only*. Petitioned the King, myself. If you know that bit of history, Senor, you must also know my acts of charity were legendary."

"I didn't, Senor Almonaster, and hope you won't hold it against me—*here in my own home.*"

"*Your home?* Not quite. I believe the Senor pays rent to the State of Louisiana?"

I shrugged and continued, "What is with you people? What gives you the right to show up at any hour of the day or night? Ever heard of ringing a doorbell or calling ahead? Lucky I don't have a heart condition. On second thought, I *do* have a heart condition!"

"My daughter, whose feelings are easily bruised, tells me she was insulted by someone in this apartment. I've come to defend her honor."

"I see. And you came all the way from *where* to tell me this?"

"Just across the Place d'Armes. My remains are entombed in the St. Louis Cathedral. Since I paid to rebuild it after the great fires of 1788, that was the least Fr. Antonio de Sedella could do. Given that I used to own all the land and buildings around the square, I find it difficult to leave the area."

"So that *was* the Baroness Pontalba who broke in here a few weeks ago?"

"Broke in, Senor? My daughter has no need to break in." He rocked back on his well-heeled boots. "Since neither the State nor the City seems to give a fig, Micaela and I take turns watching over our properties." His eyes appeared to water as he looked around my apartment. "It's not been easy."

"Nor for me. Try living with an amateur saxophonist playing "The Pink Panther" under your balcony 10 hours a day."

"Take it up with the State. I'm not here to listen to your complaints. I'm here to seek satisfaction for a great insult to my Micaela."

"Insult? By me? I think not, Sir."

"I didn't say it was you, Senor. I've thrown down the gauntlet at this foul-mouthed Williams hombre and challenged him to a duel."

"A duel? Are you putting me on, Senor Roxas?"

"It's Almonaster y Roxas, if you don't mind. I may not have dueled anyone for a couple hundred years and might appear to be a bit out of shape to you," he admitted, "but it's in my blood and dueling techniques are easily recalled when it's a question of family honor." He raised his blade high and wiggle-wagged it, hoping to snatch a menacing glint from the afternoon sun.

"Let me get this straight," I said, all but laughing in his face. "The Baroness Pontalba's Daddy is challenging Tennessee Williams to a duel and where is it going to take place?"

"Right here, Senor. Right where the detestable curr . . ." His last few words were drowned out by the sound of shattering glass coming from my bedroom.

"As ah took mah leave, so do ah make mah arrival," Tennessee Williams proclaimed, as he entered the foyer. "And bein' a gentleman of manners, I have decided to accept this silly invitation. Alas, all I could find to duel with was this ole' umbrella from "Iguana" and this cute little fake pistol from "Rose Tattoo.""

"Senor, how would you react if you heard someone had called your only daughter 'an old slut claiming to be the Baroness Pontalba'—when *she was* the Baroness Pontalba?"

"Stella by stawa! When put in such a straight forward manner, a style to which ah admit, ahm not entirely comfortable with, and comin' from someone who appears to be credible as you, Sir—ah mean jus' look at that mornin' coat! Those shiny boots! That great big mean-lookin' soword! And yoah plumed hat! Foah the fust tahm in a verah long tahm, ahm at a complete loss foah wuds."

Roxas turned to me, confusion creasing his scarred face. "I have no idea what that man just said. Could you translate, Senor?"

"I think maybe Mr. Williams is working up to an apology," I whispered from the side of my mouth. "That would mean you could call off the duel, right?"

Before Roxas could answer, Tennessee rambled on with his introspective riff. "It's jus' that youah daughtah—and I no longah have reason to believe she isn't youah daughtah, has heretofore never seemed to be a credible figah to me. I pride mah self on writin' about real people, and givin' them realistic dialogue that replicates the way real people talk about real problems. Your daughtah, if she hadn't been so rude about mah bein' an illegal tenant in her precious buildin' durin' mah yeaz of impecuniosity, ah might not have taken so painful an offense. Ah admit, when cornered or made to feel ashayemed, ah can be—well there's no other word foah it—and, mahnd ya', this is not a wud in mah normal lexicon—ah can be, and have been, a cunt."

Again, Roxas looked to me for some kind of explanation. I thought best to give it a shot. "Mr. Williams, if I may jump in here? Could you just say to this nice man that you're sorry for calling his daughter and old whore, and promise not to call her that again? Is that so difficult for you?"

"Well, pardonnez-moi, Miss Yankee Buttinski! Ahm getting' there as fast as ah cayan. And to clarifah yoah mendacity, I called her a slut, not a whoah."

A gust of wind sneaked over the dining room transom, bringing with it the now familiar whiff of sulfur and Violet Musk and behold—the perfectly coiffed and snooded Baroness Pontalba stood before us.

"I've been waiting impatiently on the gallery, Poppa, fully hoping to see Mr. Williams carried away on a stretcher, his white linen suit stained crimson. But now it feels like it's getting ready to storm. What's the hold up?"

"If I may?" I gestured to Roxas and Williams, then turned to the Baroness. "In an effort to save unnecessary bloodshed on all sides, Mr. Williams has been verbally laboring to draft an eloquent, profoundly lyrical apology to you, Micaela."

"Oh? Is this so, Papa?" y Roxas shrugged, indicating, 'if that's what the man says.'

"Suitable for publication—after a coupla' rewrites," Williams added, bowing low.

His gesture, in truth, a deeply felt genuflection, seemed so welcomed by both the Baroness and her Father, all tension immediately evaporated from the room. They smiled and nodded to Williams, then to each other. "Apology accepted," they pronounced, in chorus. It was truly a magical moment for me and the best example of diplomacy in action I'd witnessed in years.

"Ah am truly sorry for my intemperate wuds," Williams said as he reached for both their hands. "Now, let's all go 'round the cornah to Tujaques." He put his arms through theirs. "This tired ole' c-word needs one a' Dalt's gin Martinis."

"And I might have a Cuban cigar," said y Roxas.

"What do you suppose was on Monsieur Holloway's mind," the Baroness whispered to Williams, "piling all that tacky, mis-matched furniture into these elegant rooms?"

A crash of thunder and a flash of lightening right out of Götterdämmerung made me flinch and look to the gallery. When I turned back, all three were gone, leaving no trace of sulfur, only heavenly Violet Musk.

Uncle Walt's Head

Geoffrey wrote that it all began in Intercourse, a West Hollywood bar and restaurant, one Sunday evening when Leslie Grindstone, his hard-drinking friend, bragged about stumbling across a cache of secret documents while cleaning out a storage closet adjoining Walt Disney's private office, which the studio maintained as memorial to its beloved founder.

Les claimed that somehow, word of his discovery reached his supervisor by the next day, which resulted in his being summarily fired. But their mutual friend, Peter Bonwit told Geoffrey a different story. Peter, who worked as a production manager at Disney and claimed to know *everybody*, said Les was dismissed for sloppy work, taking too many sick days and falsifying overtime on his timecard. Knowing Les as Geoffrey did, it wasn't difficult to accept Peter's version.

So when Les called Geoffrey Monday morning, sounding cold-sober, cogent and anxious that he had been believed about the secret documents the night before, Geoffrey was in no hurry to give him that. Geoffrey had his own, much more serious event to report, but Les was too preoccupied to listen.

"I almost wished I hadn't said anything about the Disney thing," Les prattled on, "since you think I'm a big lush, no matter what I say." He paused to give Geoffrey time to refute this, but he didn't. "What I neglected to tell you is that I Xeroxed some of those papers and one of them has an address on it."

"Dear Les! What you won't do to gain credibility!"

"What's that supposed to mean?"

"You have to admit it is your most far-out story yet?"

"To think I was about to ask you to store them in your safety deposit box. No fucking way."

"Oh, get over it, Les. If I insulted you, that wasn't my intention." In truth, Geoffrey had to admit he was being disingenuous for, if insult wasn't his intention, what was?

At this point in Geoffrey's narrative, he takes a labyrinthine, not entirely selfless detour. Seems a couple of years prior, after Geoffrey had rescued Les for the umpteenth time and let him stay in his guest room until he got back on his feet, Les arrived from work late one evening with tiny red flecks on his shirt and necktie, claiming Jesus' blood had splattered through his computer screen! Les was certain it was a sure sign from God, though as an apostate son of a Mennonite minister, he wasn't *that* sure.

When Geoffrey pointed out that the spots looked more like red ink and that perhaps someone's correction pen had exploded, Les shook his head angrily. Geoffrey reminded him that real blood coagulates and turns brown quickly which caused Les to storm off to his room mumbling "Fuck you," over and over. Next morning, Les made no reference whatsoever to the "Christ's blood" incident. Nor did Geoffrey.

Now, years later, here again was Les on the phone shouting, "Go fuck yourself! You think you know everything about everything, Geoffrey," he ranted. "You don't know diddley-squat about this, and now you never will. Fuck you! Fuck you! Fuck you!" he screamed and slammed the receiver down. Geoffrey had never heard Les being quite so vituperative or profane.

Because Geoffrey had his own incredible story to tell regarding what had happened after he'd left Intercourse on Sunday evening, he started to dial Les back, then had second thoughts. "He'll see it on the local news," he mused aloud, "or he won't." It would be quite in character for Les, who was something of a news junkie, to have already seen the report and, out of spite, make no mention of it.

Despite having known each other for twenty years, their on-again, off-again friendship was something less than idyllic, factored by an assortment of uncontrollable elements of which Les' drinking bouts headed the list. Conversely, Geoffrey's penchant for keeping his head in the sand about the issue, ran a close second. On two occasions, Les' boozing had so alarmed Geoffrey, he stopped talking to him altogether, hoping the cold-shoulder technique would bring him to his senses, but even that strategy proved to be futile.

After several weeks of surreptitiously checking on each other's wellbeing, they had reconnected and hammered out a detente of sorts. Geoffrey would occasionally join Les at the neighborhood bar, hoping his display of moderation would set an example, which strategy proved even more ineffective. Les, for his part, promised never to get behind the wheel after two drinks, but who knew?

Their resumed socializing was centered around Geoffrey's efforts to appear sanguine as he watched Les tilt back three or four vodkas-on-the rocks and Les' ability to appear coherent and unbiased while passing along the latest in studio gossip. To hear Les tell it, working at Disney provided endless fodder for gossip-merchants. And gossip is where their conversation had migrated that Sunday evening when an urgency crept into Les' voice. He pulled Geoffrey close and whispered, "The rumors about Walt Disney are true."

"What rumors? What are you talking about?"

"Walt Disney's head is preserved in a cryogenic tank stored in a secret lab somewhere in Hollywood."

Mellowed by his second Chardonnay, Geoffrey's reply wasn't particularly dismissive. "I'd always heard it was his whole body, not just his head."

"You heard wrong," Les sniffed. "I've seen the pictures."

"Pictures? Actual photographs? You saw photographs of Disney's frozen head?" Geoffrey's tone couldn't freight another ounce of skepticism.

75

"Not so loud," Les hushed him. "Well, maybe it was more of a sketch," he allowed and faked a yawn to cover his retrenching. "But it was a very detailed sketch. You know how good the Disney people are."

At that moment, Conrad Behr and Patryk Ryker, two lovers whose ostentatious manner gave new meaning to the word, cornered them. Acquaintances of Geoffrey's, defiantly nouveau riche, Conrad and Patryk's great pleasure was being able to brag about their latest acquisition of cars, clothes, jewelry, furniture and pedigreed pets. Each time Geoffrey met up with them, he wondered how their smallish hands and slender wrists could support that much hammered gold.

"Geoffrey darling!" Conrad cooed," I just said to Patryk, it had to be you—only P.R. flacks hold such animated conversations in public."

"And this is your friend—don't tell me—Wes, right?" Patryk asked and before Geoffrey could correct him, added, "Feel free to buy us a drink."

"Help us celebrate," Conrad giggled. "Escrow just closed on The Merced Building."

"Our art deco property on Greene Street in Pasadena?" Patryk elaborated, with that Southern Debutante habit of ending every statement with a question mark.

"It's Les," Les said.

"How's that?" Patryk asked. "The music's so loud in here."

"My name is Les, not Wes," he growled, emptying his vodka in one gulp. "Sounds like you two should be the ones buying the drinks."

Neither gave any indication of having heard him and, in tandem, signaled the bartender for another round.

"So, Geoffrey," Conrad inquired, "Any of your clients working on any movies they could put our Rolls in?"

"Or our new Bentley?" added Patryk. "Wait 'til you see it, Hon. You're going to cream your jeans—original paint job—aubergine. Divine!"

The bartender placed a fresh round in front of them. "Twenty eight dollars, please," he declared, looking to Les for payment.

"If only you'd just sold a multi-million dollar property," Geoffrey snickered.

"Cheers," Conrad and Patryk raised their glasses. "Here's to shrewd investments and early retirement." With that, they kissed full on the mouth.

"And hustling paupers to pick up the tab," Les muttered.

"You're with Disney, aren't you?" Conrad asked, not really looking for an answer, but paving the way for Patryk's next bragging point.

"We just bought a block of Disney stock," Patryk explained. "I guess you could say we're paying your salary now."

If slow burns could produce heat, Les' glass would have melted into molten syrup. "I left Disney over a month ago—to freelance." He glared at Geoffrey to keep quiet. "Word around the lot," he allowed through a cobra smile, "is that Disney stock is on its way down the toilet—big time. Couldn't think of a better time to cash in and 'ankle the lot', as they say in *Variety*."

Geoffrey had to hand it to Les. He'd sunk the knife with surgical precision. Conrad and Patryk we're in high dudgeon.

"Who told you that? Are you sure? How long ago was that? Did you know this, Geoffrey? Why didn't you call us? We could have made an informed decision. I had a gut feeling that broker was trading on his looks more than the facts. Don't blame me, Conrad. You're the one with the hots for that cock-tease. This could push our retirement back by five years. We're going home now. Make a few calls. Rest assured, heads will roll."

They left their drinks untouched and high-tailed their way out of the bar.

"You owe me big-time, Geoffrey."

"I was about to say the same to you," he sniffed as the two erupted in laughter. "You could get into serious trouble lying about something as sacred as Disney stock."

"Fuck 'em if they can't take a joke." Les signaled the bartender for another round.

Geoffrey put his hand over his glass. "One more and I'll have to be hospitalized. What were you saying before we were so rudely interrupted?"

"I think I just fell in love." Les gestured toward the dance floor where a buffed and sweating black man was lumbering about, giving lie to the legend that his gene pool gave him an edge on rhythm.

"What about Disney's head?" Geoffrey persisted.

A rail-thin, heavily rouged queen floated past them, pausing long enough to interject, "So right, sweet lips! Uncle Walt gave great head. I know from first-hand experience," he added triumphantly, and disappeared into the crowd.

"Friend of yours?" Geoffrey asked.

"Of course not," Les frowned. "I'm off to the little boy's. See if you can scare up another round while I'm gone."

"Not unless you give me your car keys."

"You are one pompous prick," he snarled and gave Geoffrey the finger, then followed the black man into the toilet.

Weary of fretting about what would happen if Les got another DUI, Geoffrey decided he'd had it for the evening. He signaled the bartender he was leaving, told him to inform Les only if he asked about Geoffrey's whereabouts, left a generous tip and set out on a leisurely walk home.

It was one of those balmy, cool nights that make the stresses of living in LA worthwhile. Geoffrey considered his neighborhood to be one of the safest in L.A. except when invaded by the heartypartyers steering their SUVs and neon-under-lighted Corvettes off Sunset Boulevard and down its residential streets. It was de rigueur that their windows remain wide open, stereos blasting at full decibel while the driver roared at someone over his cell phone. Geoffrey was sure one of these days something hideous would result from these Road Warriors striving to impress their Fast Food Princesses.

There's no traffic signal where Norton Way dead-ends into Sweetzer Avenue, and the overhanging foliage is so dense, it blocks the streetlamps. At night, the blind spots are so bad, unless one proceeds cautiously or knows the intersection, it's easy to cruise through the stop sign, unaware it exists.

A black Range Rover, its headlights off, sailed phantomlike down the middle of Sweetzer. Apparently, its driver didn't see or didn't care about the rust-brown Datsun making a wide, right turn off Norton. When, at the last second, each vehicle swerved to miss the other, the Range Rover proved the sturdier of the two. With a horrifying crunch, the passenger side of the Datsun was stowed in, which sent the vehicle rolling over.

What happened next was so unreal, Geoffrey found it difficult to describe without becoming nauseous at each recounting. A round-faced Hispanic woman in the front passenger seat of the Datsun, looking to be in her early twenties, was leaning out of the window, joyfully shouting epithets at the world. When the road-hogging Rover suddenly appeared, the young woman directed her curses toward it and continued to rant as the Datsun rolled over, landed first on it side and then on its roof, which held but a moment before collapsing under the weight of the chassis. The window frame became a guillotine and decapitated the woman mid-curse, which sent her head rolling, like a bewigged soccer ball, directly towards Geoffrey. He swore she was still screaming when her head stopped inches from where he stepped off the curb, but he couldn't be absolutely certain.

Immediately, the Range Rover tried to back up, as if to get away. Geoffrey ran to it, jumped on its front bumper and plastered himself against it like an outsized hood ornament. "Stop this car now!" he bellowed. "Are you mad! trying to leave the scene of an accident?"

The driver glared through the tinted glass as he tried to decide whether to slam it in gear, speed away and throw Geoffrey off in the doing or make it look like he was backing off the pancaked Datsun. While he wavered, his female companion grabbed for the keys and, after a brief struggle, hurled them out the window. When they hit the ground, they set off the Rovers's ear-shattering alarm system, adding to the bedlam. For an instant, it looked like the driver was going to punch Geoffrey out, but his girlfriend restrained him and the Rover stayed put until the police arrived.

The rest of the evening was a blur of emergency vehicles, TV news cameras, sheriff's cars, acetylene torches, Jaws of Life, hysterical survivors, and dozens of onlookers, mostly Russian immigrant Seniors standing around in their bathrobes. The image of a sweet-faced crone tenderly placing her fringed shawl over the severed head was not one Geoffrey would soon forget. Minutes later, the object was noticed by one of the officers who immediately shouted for an assistant to remove it. The young man apologized to the old lady as he handed the blood-soaked shawl back to her. Her shrug seemed to say, "It's just a piece of cloth", as she made the sign of the cross.

Geoffrey's ID was checked and recorded and he was asked to repeat his story several times along with the other witnesses, two men who had the misfortune to be walking their schnauzers at that horrendous moment. The dogs had become hysterical at the sight of the decapitated head, forcing the younger man to haul them back home. When he reappeared, Geoffrey exchanged cards with him and his partner and learned their names were Franklin and Barney. They corroborated for the police, as best they could, what each had witnessed.

It was after 2:00 when the investigating officers finally released everyone. Geoffrey offered to buy Franklin and Barney a nightcap, but they reminded him last call was 1:45. When Franklin, the older one, whispered that Barney was AA, Geoffrey mumbled an apology, adding that he was in such shock, he could easily drink a fifth of cognac himself, were it available.

All that was then.

Just now, Les had slammed his receiver down before Geoffrey could recount any of it. For the time being, the possibility of seeing another decapitated head, no matter how famous or well-iced, held little appeal for Geoffrey.

Very little work got done over the next few days. The phone rang continuously, with reporters and newsrooms wanting follow up and further verification on exactly what had been witnessed. They couldn't seem to get enough of the gory details. Geoffrey, Barney and Franklin had been quoted at length in the newspapers and several of the news channels shared a sound byte of Geoffrey saying, "Horrible" like a hairy soccer ball landing at my feet," which they played round-the-clock.

By Wednesday, there was no way Les could *not* have heard about the catastrophe and Geoffrey's involvement with it. But like most alcoholics whose emotional pendulum swings from petulance to petulance, Les never made the slightest move to contact him. In contrast, Geoffrey heard from Barney and Franklin several times a day, wanting advice on how to handle the avalanche of media calls. Beyond suggesting they stop answering the phone altogether and let their answering machine do its work, he was at a loss himself. By Thursday, the two had had enough and escaped to a friend's villa in Laguna Beach, first stopping by the WeHo Sheriff's station to inform the officers of their whereabouts. Geoffrey envied them.

Inevitably there we would be a hearing and trial, and they'd all be subpoenaed and deposed by all sides. It made Geoffrey wonder what the fates we're up to, what lesson he should be learning from this? And, he certainly had second thoughts about not having stayed on at Intercourse with Les that night.

A full week passed when Geoffrey received a message that Les had called his office and made a point of insisting he didn't wish to speak to him directly. "Tell Geoffrey to have one of that platoon of employees of his call and give me an update".

Geoffrey took that as Les-speak for, 'If he really doesn't want to talk to me ever again, don't confront me directly with the news.' More than likely it meant Les was feeling commiserative and apologetic, but Geoffrey let another two days pass. He called early Wednesday morning, hoping to catch him off guard and sober, but Les surprised him by answering on the first ring.

"I hope this is one of your minions and not you?"

Off guard, Les wasn't. As to sober, Geoffrey could only hope. "It's me." Geoffrey put a smile in his voice. "You must be sick of seeing me on the news by now?" Les made no reply. "Truthfully, I'm still having nightmares"

"You witnessed an accident. It was bad. They're all bad. You'll get over it. Don't wallow in it" Les never sounded more sensible.

"When that woman's head rolled . . ."

". . . it was horrible, like a hairy soccer ball landing at my feet." His joy at mimicking Geoffrey seemed to invigorate him. "Jesus, Geoff, the whole city knows that line. I hear the *Pet Shop Boys* are setting it to music. They'll be dancing to it at *The Factory* by the weekend."

"To quote a former friend of mine, Fuck you, fuck you, and fuck you."

"If I insulted you, Geoffrey, I'm sorry. That wasn't my intention."

"Touché. Are we even?"

"I wouldn't go quite that far," Les giggled nervously. "Listen, my savings are about to run out—I just learned that Disney is denying my Unemployment. This free-lance shit isn't cutting it. I need to lay hands on some money, fast."

"You asking for a loan?"

"Not exactly. Let me finish."

"The IRS is putting me through another audit and I'm not in a position . . ."

"You always say that, Geoffrey. Relax. I'm not hitting you up yet."

"I might be able to scrape up a couple hundred."

"Thanks. I may need it. Later. What would be a big help is if you could put me in touch with anyone who has contacts at the National Enquirer or any of the tabloids."

"Do I get to ask why?"

"Yes, but I won't answer over the phone."

"Fine. I won't mention my contacts at the National Enquirer, either." Had Geoffrey been struck deaf and dumb, he'd still be able to guess where this was going. "This related to Mr. Birdseye?"

"Not over the phone, goddam it!"

"Sorry."

"Maybe we could meet tonight—for an early supper? Have to be your treat until I'm back on my feet."

"7:30 is the soonest I could get away. French Market?"

"Perfect! I'll get there early. Find us a quiet table in the back. Please, not a word to anyone? Especially your blabber-mouthed assistant, Robbie."

"And you call me a drama queen."

"Don't start," he grunted, though he sounded genuinely humbled. "Leave me a message if you're going to be late."

Geoffrey elected not to mention the appointment to Robbie or have him put it on his calendar, so he nearly forgot about the date. But, despite his frantic day, he was only a few minutes late when the Maitre d' led him back to Les. They hugged tentatively and, before Geoffrey could sit down, Les handed him a large black envelope.

"Ahh! Black. Always inconspicuous."

"Fuck you. Now listen." Les looked over his shoulder nervously. "When I give the signal, go to the men's room, lock yourself in one of the stalls and then you can open it."

"How about we order first? I'm starving."

"I thought you'd be burning with curiosity."

"I am, but curiosity is proportionate to my blood sugar level. I had two cups of coffee for breakfast and a tofu burger for lunch—while driving between studios. Right now, I could eat old shoes." Geoffrey signaled the waiter and ordered his usual broiled chicken and fruit plate. As if to remind who was picking up the tab, Les ordered a shrimp cocktail, a sirloin steak, a baked potato *and* French fries along with a second Bud Lite.

When the waiter was out of earshot, Les resumed. "There's a total of six documents in there. Three are photographs, two are technical blueprints and one is a floor plan of the building."

Geoffrey was too hungry to concentrate. "What building?"

"The lab, for Christ's sake!" When heads turned at the next table, Les realized he was shouting. "The place where he's . . . you know . . . stored," he retreated, soto voce.

"I'm about to faint." Geoffrey handed the envelope back to Les. "Keep this until I get some food in me." He signaled the busboy. "Would you please bring us some crackers or bread and butter—anything until our food arrives?" Les looked as if he might bolt but necessity and hunger intervened.

By the time they finished their meal, he was about to order his fourth beer.

"Why is this so important to you?" Geoffrey asked. "Even if this story is true, and I certainly have my reservations about it, what do you hope to do with it?"

"After the shitty way the Disney people treated me, I think I deserve some kind of compensation—a proper slice of the pie. But nobody's going to hand it to me. Or hire me back with a fat raise and a pension. Think about it. Everybody says the tabloids pay big money for this kind of stuff. I could make a nice piece of change—pay off all the bills and have enough left to move back to Maui. Not have to worry for a long, long while. I'm happy to give you a taste if you decide to help.

"What kind of money are you looking for?"

"You tell me? Couple a hundred thousand? Quarter of a million doesn't seem unreasonable." He finished off his beer and signaled for the waiter to bring him another.

"Where did you come up with those figures?"

"A friend who works in hair and makeup at Fox. Claims *The Star* has her on retainer to give them the skinney on all the celebrities she does."

"Gives new meaning to only her hairdresser knows for sure," Geoffrey winced. "However, repeating gossip and handing over stolen photographs are two vastly different things."

"So you're not interested?" he huffed.

"Intrigued is a better word. But I won't take any money and I won't knowingly break the law."

"Mr. Clean all of a sudden," he sniffed. "What about all those dope deals you've pulled off down at Fifth and Alvarado?"

"Scoring an occasional lid of grass for my clients is not pulling off a dope deal. Besides, you never complained when I gave you a taste."

"Been off Mary Jane for months," Les shrugged. "But I sure could use a puff about now."

"Well, I don't have any." He pointed to the envelope. "You still want me to look at this or not?"

"That's why we're here. Just go to the men's room and do it."

"Wouldn't my car be safer?"

"No way. They have security cameras all over the place. Can't take the chance."

So it was that Geoffrey found himself locked in a stall in the men's room at the French Market, straddling a commode to make it look like he was actually using it. As he unsealed the envelope, he heard the sound of two men in the adjoining stall, taking turns at oral sex. His first glimpse of the intricately detailed sketches, slightly blurred for being copies, reinforced the absurdity of his situation and gave new meaning to the expression, 'Giving head.'

The illustrations, stamped 'TOP SECRET' in orange at the right margin, were more bizarre than Les had hinted. They depicted a large metal and glass tank suspended over a girdered platform at the center of a tiled room. The unmistakable outline of a human face could be seen through the porthole riveted into its gleaming surface. The vessel was flanked by an assortment of stainless steel and aluminum canisters from which all manner of hoses and valves flowed.

The omission of signatures and dates, purportedly a house rule for all Disney's artists, made it impossible to determine whether this was an actual construction or merely renderings for a 'Mad-scientist' movie set. Most intriguing: someone had scrawled *1426 Morningside Court* in pencil at the bottom of the electrical schematic.

"That was awesome," a voice in the adjoining stall whispered.

"For me, too," the other agreed. "What's your name?"

"Rather not say. That's my lover I'm sitting with. He gets real suspicious."

"Whatever. See ya' 'round."

Geoffrey stuffed everything back in the envelope, tucked it under his arm and unlatched the door. Two men, considerably older and heavier than he'd imagined, were drying their hands at the brass sinks. As they exited, the younger one said, "Where the fuck did he come from?"

"Must have been in the next booth."

"Probably got his jollys for the year."

"Trailer trash," Geoffrey mumbled as he wet his hands and ran them through his salt and pepper hair.

When he returned to the table, Les was glaring in agitation. "What the hell took you so long?"

"Les, that's offensive and totally unnecessary."

"That leather queen, the one with the beard that came out ahead of you—he's notorious. Were you doing the nasty with him?"

"Good God, no! Public sex is not my thing, and even if it was, he'd be the last one I'd do it with."

Mollified for the moment, Les snatched the black envelope. "What'd you think?"

"That address on Morningside Court . . . have you checked it out?

"Yes. 30's Deco building, in fairly good shape, but it's all bricked up. According to the sign by the loading dock, it used to be a facility for film preservation."

"Interesting." Geoffrey signaled for the check and put down cash. "I guess there's no harm in taking a look?"

Les perked up. For real? "When did you have in mind?"

"How about now? We'll go in my car."

"Now you're sounding like the Geoffrey Putnam I used to know and love."

Geoffrey steered his Mercedes east along Sunset, turned right onto Morningside Court and came to a stop behind The Cinerama Dome. The only thing in view was a vast, empty parking lot, with a lone, unoccupied attendant's booth crouched in the middle.

"This is the 1400 block of Morningside—so where's this Deco building you were talking about?"

"Shit!" Les belched. "I must have been looking on the wrong side of Sunset. Sorry."

Morningside was a narrow, one way street. Geoffrey had the choice of pulling ahead into the parking lot, which, according to the sign at the gate, operated on the honor system on weekdays, or taking a left which would put them onto Vine Street.

"Something doesn't smell quite right," Geoffrey sniffed. "What year was the Dome built?"

"How the hell should I know?" Les yawned. "And what's that got to do with anything, anyway?"

"We'll be sitting ducks in the parking lot," Geoffrey mumbled to himself. "Let's see if we can't find a space on Vine while we figure this out."

"Disney died in '66," Les offered. "Recall it was just before Christmas, if that means anything."

As luck would have it, Geoffrey found a spot immediately south of the Sunset & Vine intersection. "I think this requires a bit of close-up snooping," he said, as he waved for Les to get out of the car so he could lock it. "Here, take my briefcase—there's a flashlight in it. I'll carry these folders. Makes us look official. If anybody asks, we're with Allstate, checking out a damage claim."

"Cool," Les answered admiringly. "You're really getting into this, aren't you?"

"Who doesn't like a good mystery?" Geoffrey chuckled. "Follow me. Something caught my eye just before we turned toward Vine."

"I didn't see anything."

"That's because I drank iced tea and you had how many beers?"

"You gonna' start on that shit again?"

"I never stopped. Look, if Uncle Walt is indeed stored here, there's bound to be security cameras everywhere." Geoffrey pointed at a lean-to type structure attached to the back of the Dome. Covered with ivy, both of them nearly missed seeing the non-descript metal door with a bronze plaque welded onto it. "Flashlight," Geoffrey commanded.

"Look at that," he marveled. "Built 1963 as a joint venture for the Cinerama Corporation and Pacific Theatres. Designed by Welton Becket Associates, Pasadena, CA."

"There's no handle on the door. Must house A/C equipment or high voltage electrical stuff," Les ventured.

"Or that's what they want us to think." Geoffrey shook his head. "If it's high voltage, where's the 'Danger' sign?"

Les pointed to a tiny button set in the casement. "Look," he mouthed. A speaker, the size of a 50¢ piece, was mounted just above it.

"Sweet," Geoffrey mused. "What do you say?"

"We've come this far . . ." Les shrugged and pushed the button. When nothing resulted, he pushed it again and held it for a few seconds. Suddenly, the speaker crackled to life. "You are trespassing on private property. You have 20 seconds to enter the voice code or leave before alarms are sounded." Les flashed Geoffrey his 'What the fuck?' look.

The mechanical voice continued, "17, 16, 15, 14,"

"Worth a try," Geoffrey whispered and leaned to the tiny speaker. "1, 4, 2, 6" he enunciated but the countdown continued, "11, 10, 9 . . ."

Inspired, Les spat out, "Morningside Court! 1426 Morningside Court!" Immediately, the countdown stopped—a series of buzzes and clicks followed and the door slid open, revealing an unlighted metal box not much larger than an upended casket.

"Holy shit," Les mumbled.

The mechanical voice resumed, "Door closes in 10 seconds—9, 8, 7 . . ."

Geoffrey shoved Les inside and crowded beside him as the door whooshed closed, plunging them into total darkness. Immediately, it began descending.

"You've got the flashlight, Geoff. For Christ's sake, turn it on."

"No I don't. Must have set it down after we . . ."

"Fuck. And I left my lighter in your car."

The coffin continued to descend.

"How far down can it go?" Les asked, clearly terrified.

"Three—maybe four stories—earthquake protection?" he guessed, trying to sound calm and informed. "Whatever happens, remember we're with Allstate."

"Like I know shit about insurance," Les groaned as the box came to a halt. Behind them, a door slid open, bathing them in a flood of blinding white light.

"Are—you—the guys—from—the—TV—repair?" a tiny voice, with a pronounced stutter, asked.

They turned to see an albino child, not more than 9 or 10, sitting behind an ordinary metal desk, dwarfed by a dozen security monitors arranged in the wall behind him. Half of them appeared to be out of order. Dumbstruck, neither one replied.

The albino boy pressed on. "Because you didn't show up, my Daddy—went to get—to get some—other guys. My Daddy left me . . . in charge," he said, with a hint of pride.

"You're all alone here?" Geoffrey asked at the same moment Les blurted out, "We're from Allstate."

"Allstate TV repair," Geoffrey expanded.

"Tool kit," Les said as he held up the briefcase.

"They told Daddy you'd be here by 18:00 hours. What took you so long?"

Geoffrey kicked Les' ankle. "Trouble with our van."

"Pileup on the freeway," Les embroidered, with a wink. "What's your Daddy's name, little guy?"

"Our Supervisor forgot to write it down," Geoffrey said, waving the manila folders.

"Daddy is Kolzak. I'm Kolzak, too."

"Nice. So do we call you, Little Kolzak?"

"No, Silly. I am called Konstantine—Konstantine Kolzak. Now, you better get busy and fix the televisions."

"We'll give it our best shot," Geoffrey declared, but his look indicated otherwise. Recovering, he declared, "We'll need to get behind that wall, Kolzak. Can you show us where the door is?"

"Kolzak can." He pointed to an oval-shaped box resting on the desk—a blue halo radiated from its base. "But one of you . . . guys has to put your . . . hand in here, first. Daddy says that's . . . SOP."

Les hesitated, but on Geoffrey's nod, inserted his hand. "Your Daddy must be very proud of you," Les muttered. When he withdrew it, a panel to the right of the monitors glided open.

Instantly assaying the situation, Geoffrey raised his brow as sign for Les to pay close attention. "Look, you stay out here . . . and keep an eye on the . . . . screens. That way you can call out the *numbers* while I make the . . . *calibrations* . . . on the back. I don't think our Walkies are going to work this far underground."

"Walkies? What Walkies? Oh, right. Got it . . . G." He tossed the briefcase to him. "Here's the tool kit. Good luck," he smirked.

The Albino boy opened a drawer, removed a plastic card from its protective shield and handed it to Geoffrey. "You need this, Mister. You need to swipe it to get in *and* swipe it to get out. So don't . . . don't lose it."

"Thank you, Konstantine . . . Mr. Kolzak. I won't." With a mock salute, Geoffrey strode through the opening and felt a twinge of claustrophobia as it slid shut behind him. To his left, a panel marked 'Security Monitors' loomed, with its ubiquitous card-swipe lock. When it refused to open after three tries, he figured the boy must have given him the wrong card. Looking around, he saw a second door marked "Authorized Personnel Only Beyond This Point."

Not since age ten, when he'd jimmied the lock on his Aunt Hattie's pie safe, had Geoffrey perceived anything so tempting! On a hunch, he swiped the card and, miracle of miracles, the panel raised, guillotine fashion. Suddenly, there he was, easy as that, standing in a giant chamber which looked amazingly like the drawings. The exception being that the walls were sheathed in brushed aluminum instead of white tile and a network of steel trusses that looked to be recent additions, reinforced the vaulted ceiling.

Geoffrey was surprised by how quiet it was—no throbbing pumps, no hissing valves or gurgling pipes. Absolute silence prevailed. And, exactly as in the renderings, there was the stainless steel and glass vat suspended from cables in the center of the chamber. "Incredible! Absolutely incredible!" he exclaimed as he unsnapped the briefcase and removed his Minolta. "Who'd ever believe it?"

Out in the security area, Les paced back and forth, yelling directions at the wall of monitors. "Nothing yet on number 4," he called out. "Try checking the audio input franit again."

A red light on the desk phone blinked, accompanied by an ominous chirping. Konstantine picked it up immediately. "Hallo. Yes, Ludmil. Yes, they are here. Oh, I see. That is good. I will tell them. Goodbye, Ludmil."

Soon as he hung up, Les demanded to know, "Who was Ludmil and why had he called?"

"Ludmil is my Daddy. On his way back from Laguna. Said he'll be here in a few minutes. He wants you to wait."

Despite the frigid temperature, Les commenced to sweat and pointed to the sliding door. "Could you open it, please? I need to explain this to G. He hates surprises."

"Only one . . . person at a time allowed . . . back there."

Foiled for the moment, Les resumed yelling at the monitors. "Did you hear that, G? The boss is on his way back. He'll be here in a few minutes. We'd better have these friggin' TVs fixed before then."

Unfortunately, Geoffrey heard none of it. Mesmerized, he crept around to the other side of the vat and there it was, in all its grotesque glory: Walt Disney's head—or something quite resembling it, slowly twisting about like a giant squid in crystal-clear corn syrup, twice magnified by the convex glass in the porthole.

Geoffrey brought the Minolta viewfinder to his eye. "Could this be any more creepy?" he wondered aloud and pressed the shutter button. But nothing happened. He pressed again and a third time, and still it wouldn't function. "Damn! Double-damn!" he cursed and shook the camera but it was no use—apparently the batteries were dead. "How can this be?" he implored the face in the vat, then ransacked his briefcase, frantically searching for replacements. "That lying SOB, Robbie! Told me he charged them after he borrowed it last week!"

A bald, black-suited bear of a man burst into the chamber, brandishing a stun gun. "Alright, hands over your head!" he bellowed. "Get down on the floor, NOW! All the way down, cocksucker! One false move, and I'll burn your balls off with this thing."

Offering no resistance whatsoever, Geoffrey sank to his knees, fell forward and hit his face on the concrete floor which broke off a front cap. He wondered how the evening could possibly become any more surreal.

"Who the fuck are you and how the fuck did you and your asshole buddy get in here?"

"Allthate—Thecurity Repairth," Geoffrey lisped.

"Don't give me that crap, Mister. Maybe you can bullshit my little Konstantin, but you can't bullshit me." He planted his foot in the small of Geoffrey's back and reached for the Minolta.

"You mutht be Mr. Kolthak," Geoffrey whimpered. "I wathn't able to take any picturth."

"And I'm not taking any chances," Kolzak countered as he smashed the camera open and ripped the film from it. He followed this by yelling toward the corridor. "Franklyn, you stay out there and help Konstantine guard that other cocksucker. Barney, get your ass in here and make sure nothing's been fucked with."

On hearing those names, Geoffrey was sure he was hallucinating or had the answer to his surreal question—or both.

"Your boy and Franklyn have the other one under control, Ludmil," Barney said as he sauntered into the chamber. "Since you scared him to death." He glanced around the space, checked a couple of valves and hoses and proclaimed that everything seemed in order.

"Take a gander at this one," Kolzak ordered as he grabbed Geoffrey's hair and jerked his face to one side.

"Oh, my God," Barney exclaimed. "It can't be. No way!"

"What the fuck you belly-aching about?" Kolzak demanded.

"He's a friend of mine—and Franklyn's. That's Geoffrey. Geoffrey Put . . ." Barney stopped himself and took a deep breath. "Trust me, there has to be some logical explanation for this, Ludmil. Put away that stupid stun gun and let the poor man up—that is if you haven't already broken his back." He leaned over. "Are you alright, Geoffrey? You okay to move?"

"I think tho," Geoffrey sighed in mystified relief.

"Here, let me help you," Barney offered and whispered in his ear. "Don't say a word—I'll handle everything." He put his arms around Geoffrey's shoulders and pulled him to his feet. "Nothing bruised or broken, *Mr. Putin*?" he asked, pointedly.

"Juth my toof," Geoffrey answered, wobbling a bit.

"I think it's the contractor's greed and stupidity—sending Geoff and his partner out on a job as specialized as this," Barney declared. "Geoff is used to dealing with movie stars and sports figures—any number of *living and breathing* celebrities." He paused to make sure his message had hit its mark. "Knowing Geoff as I do, he was just trying to do right by his company, do his boss a favor, even though he knew he might be stepping in way over his head. Just proves, once again, no good deed goes unpunished around here."

His over-the-top speech clearly had its effect on Kolzak and put Geoffrey in such gratitude, he started to tear up. "I don't know what to thay, except I'm thorry." Warming to the subterfuge, he continued on. "I'm tho thorry. Tho, tho thorry. We thought the thurge protectors were located in thith room and . . ."

"It's okay, Geoff," Barney interrupted him and glared at Ludmil. "No need to say anymore. You've been put through enough confusion for ten technicians. Now, let's get you and your partner out of here. We'll deal with the paperwork *and recriminations* tomorrow."

"What about the monitors?" Kolzak asked as they made their way to the reception area. "What do I tell Mr. Eisner about when they're likely to get fixed?"

"Franklyn's on the case, Kolzak. He'll have them up and running in no time." Indeed, as they stepped into reception, all six dead monitors stuttered to life. "See, what'd I tell you? Franklyn deserves a bonus"

Les leaned against the wall—motionless—wide-eyed—his jaw agape.

"Daddy, I don't think those guys know what they're doing," Konstantine said, tugging at Ludmil's arm.

"Maybe they don't, Son, but they were just trying to help. Now it's time for you to go to bed. You made your Daddy very proud tonight, Konstantine."

"I'd say it's time for all of us to get some shut-eye," Franklyn suggested, quietly.

"Since Ludmil insisted on dragging us back here in his vehicle, we had to leave ours in Laguna," Barney said.

"I could drop you off in my Mertheydies . . . company van," Geoffrey offered. "It's parked right there on Vine."

"I guess that would be alright since I'm pulling a double-shift tonight," Ludmil shrugged lamely. "You guys go ahead and take a taxi back to Laguna tomorrow morning. Get a receipt—submit it to that UPM guy, Peter Bonwit. Disney'll pay for it."

"Perfect!" Barney exclaimed. "Now, let's get the heck out of here." As the four crammed into the elevator, he said to Les. "I don't believe we've actually met before."

During the short drive, first to Les' car, parked at the French Market and then to Franklyn & Barney's condo on Sweetzer, several explanations were called for and a few were given.

"Ludmil tracked us down in Laguna—where, if you remember, we went to get away," Barney offered.

"Turns out, only you and the West Hollywood police knew where we were," Franklyn clarified.

"We don't need to know how or why you crashed the facility," Barney went on, 'but rest assured, you're not the first to do it."

"Really?" was Les' trenchant response.

"But you're probably the last," Franklyn stated ominously.

"Shit! And I didn't get to see a goddamned thing," Les moaned.

"Be glad you didn't," said Barney. "And Geoffrey, be grateful your batteries were dead. If they hadn't been, it could easily be you and Les' funeral, instead."

"If you thay tho," Geoffrey shrugged. "But I have to athk you guith thomething—you theem like really dethent peopleth. If it's thuch a bad thituation, why do you thtay? What keeps you there?"

"When we first interviewed, as a team, we had no idea what we were getting into. Then, after a two month orientation period, they brought us to the Dome . . ."

" . . . in the middle of the night—blindfolded," Franklyn interjected.

"By then we already knew too much."

"And it was too late to back out. It's like the conspiracy theories over the Kennedy assassination," Franklyn continued.

"You lost me with that one," Les grumbled.

"The government counts on the truth being too outlandish for the average Joe to buy it. Same deal with Disney's head."

"And, once you've signed on, they know where you live— they know the exact whereabouts of your families . . ."

"We decided it was best to just do our job, take the money, which is very good by any standards, and keep our mouths shut," Barney concluded.

"And, just think, on the day when medical science discovers how to make it work—it will all have been worth it," Franklyn offered, with a shrug.

"Certainly worth it as far as the Disney Empire is concerned," Les sneered.

But it was Geoffrey who had the last word, "Not to menthion Uncle Walt."

Several weeks later, while his Mercedes was in the shop, Geoffrey found himself driving a rental car. Burning with curiosity (the cap on his front tooth having been restored and his blood sugar level under control) he cruised by the rear of the Cinerama Dome. Not a trace of the ivy-covered attachment remained. In its place, a giant dumpster, heaped high with movie-goer effluvia, moldered in the August heat, waiting to be hauled away.

"Sorry if we disturbed you, Uncle Walt," he whispered. "It won't happen again, I promise."

Disney Studios
Re-animation Laboratories

Electrical Engineering Schematic
For Proposed off-site laboratory
Budget Code: Birdseye
Issue Date: 1/12/64
(#1 of 6)

CAUTION: LIMITED DISTRIBUTION

!! TOP SECRET !!
!! TOP SECRET !!
!! TOP SECRET !!

1426 Morningside Court, H'wood

Baby Madeleine

It had been said that in all of Los Angeles' Mid-Wilshire district there were no more deserving parents than Prescott and Sally Sturdevant. Having survived three miscarriages and a heart-breaking full-term still-born, the thirty-something couple had all but given up their quest for a baby when Emalina Casañas, their Honduran housekeeper, suggested they give Tegucigalpa's fabled orphanages a try.

On landing in that precipitous gorge that is Toncontin Airport, the Sturdevants hailed a taxi and endured a teeth-rattling ride to *Nuestra Madre de la Luna Grande Huerfanos*, in the heart of the Red Light district. Guessing the *Americano's* humanitarian mission, the driver charged only half again the posted rate.

Sandwiched between a voodoo shop and an empanada stand, a narrow wooden staircase led to the crenellated front door of the orphanage where a gaggle of soft-spoken Maccabee nuns greeted the Sturdevants in near-perfect Spanglish. Once inside, and further niceties exchanged, their briefcase containing $12,000. in unmarked $20. bills was triple-counted and handed over to Mother Superior August Angelica. On her nod, the couple was immediately shown an extensive variety of infants.

In fact, the range proved more daunting than the Sturdevants had ever dreamed. Prepared to select from beige-skinned brunettes with hazel eyes, instead, they were confronted with scores of black babies with red hair, red babies with blonde hair, and brown babies with emerald eyes and flaxen hair. Traditional Spanish-looking infants of either gender, were in the minority.

After two-and-a-half hours of gazing into bassinettes, cribs, playpens and triple-decker bunks, Prescott suggested they should retire to their hotel and come back the next morning, refreshed and clear-headed, to continue their shopping. Sally took exception to the word, 'shopping,' but Mother August Angelica immediately comprehended Prescott's logic. "Your briefcase will be kept in the Mother's personal vault for safekeeping," she assured them.

Later, at the Hotel Alsacia, exhausted from their emotionally wrenching afternoon, Sally could find nothing good to say about the orphanage or the hotel and lapsed into conspicuous silence. Equally frustrated, Prescott ignored an empty stomach, unscrewed a bottle of rum from the honor bar and, forgoing ice-cubes, downed several warm *Cuba Libres*. He soon threw up into the Bird of Paradise growing from a cracked tile on the miniscule balcony, collapsed fully clothed onto an armchair and into the soundest sleep he'd had in months.

Awakened at 7:00 next morning by the tolling of recorded cathedral bells, and despite the lack of hot water in their shower, the lye-like soap and sand-papery towels, the couple hugged and affirmed their determination to pursue their goal with renewed enthusiasm. Their resolve was abruptly put to test by the hotel's buffet breakfast, served in a splendidly decaying banquet room just off the soon-to-be modernized lobby. The portable steam tables proffered twelve varieties of rice and beans garnished with traditional candied orchids, breaded locusts, deep-fried starlings and blackened pig's knuckles. Unable to choose from the eclectic presentation, Sally settled on a Diet-Coke and a tostada shell. Prescott braved a mug of highly touted Honduran coffee along with a hand of bananas, sliced *con leche* and immediately regretted it. Legend had it that Montezuma had never ventured this far south, but his revenge certainly had, forcing Sally to seek a flask of Caopectate at a nearby *farmacia*. When, finally it was safe for Prescott to leave the *bano de hombres*, they were more than an hour late for their return to *La Ninos Huerfanos*.

Sister Sirach, a horse-faced novitiate of indeterminate age, greeted them with a big smile and Baltimore accent beneath the roll-up door. *"Buenos dias, Senor y Senora Prescott.* We been waitin' for ya' all mornin'."

"We have a fresh batch to show ya," Sister Tobit, thirtyish and mustachioed, bragged in her unmistakable Minneapolis accent.

"Arrived early this morning from our sister orphanage in La Cieba," Sister Sirach prattled on nervously.

"It's a port city, on the Caribbean side," Sister Tobit added.

"Sailors make mischief there," Sister Sirach giggled, holding her hand over her mouth in an attempt to hide missing teeth.

"I'll bet," Prescott commented, before Sally could caution him not to say anything.

Mother August Angelica emerged from the life-sized crèche depicting the Crucifixion in plaster-of-Paris and moldering paper maché, thereby startling everyone.

"Sister Tobit—Sister Sirach," she hissed. "For shame! You'll report to my office directly before mid-morning Confessions. I'm recommending Father Magdalene assign both of you hair shirts."

The young women burst into tears and genuflected their way out of the lobby, knocking over a three-legged lamb and tearing the toga off a Roman guard as they begged God Almighty, Christ the Redeemer, The Virgin Mary, Mother August and the Sturdevants for forgiveness of their worldly transgressions. Prescott thought the moment provided him with an opportunity to ask for a discounted adoption fee, but on Sally's look, held his tongue.

Anticipating this brand of haggling, Mother August reminded him that, take home a baby or not, $2,000. of the $12,000. was the Huerfano's non-refundable processing and handling surcharge. Satisfied she'd checkmated Prescott for the moment, she hauled herself to her full 4'8" and hustled the Sturdevants to a wing they'd not visited the previous day. There, the coloration of the newly arrived La Cieba babies—uniformly Scandinavian-Octoroon—instantly elevated Sally's mood.

It wasn't until the moment when she asked to hold a boy and Prescott reached for a girl, they realized they'd never discussed which gender they were looking for.

"I assumed you wanted a girl," Prescott said, gently.

"And I thought you wanted a boy," Sally responded, choking back selfless tears.

Seizing upon their indecision, Mother August Angelica suggested, "Why not take both? I'm sure we can work out a satisfactory rate."

Sally looked at Prescott, imploringly. "Oh, could we, Press?"

"Out of the question," he said, shaking his head tic-like. "The paper work for one baby is daunting enough. Then there's inoculations, braces—college tuition!" He laid the infant girl back in her crib and turned to Mother Superior. "I'm afraid one is all we can afford."

Sally placed the boy toddler back in his crib. "Then it will be a girl."

"You're sure? You really mean that, Sally?" exclaimed Prescott, in happy astonishment.

And so it was settled. Sharing tears of joy, the couple picked a blonde, blue-eyed angel, approximately 24 months old. That done, Honduran bureaucracy demanded its mandatory hour and officials from the *Departmento de Emigracion* were summoned. When it was learned the paper work would take at least two more days, the idea of leaving the baby behind for even one night quite overwhelmed the Sturdevants. Sally beseeched the Mother Superior to assign them a sleeping alcove, and, after shrewd bartering on both sides, she agreed. Prescott taxied back to the Alsacia to fetch their belongings.

The ancient, semi-secret order of Maccabees is distinguished by its ongoing masses, celebrated twenty-four hours a day. No sooner had Sally and Prescott settled into their cubicle and on the name 'Madeleine' (fortuitously, both their maternal grandmothers shared that melodious surname), than bi-hourly summons to worship commenced. The sonorous drone of bells and barked commands, *"Aumenten y brillen, damas,"* ("Rise and shine, ladies.") reverberated through the passageways. The thrill of having baby Madeleine lying between them soon faded as the infant's squalling over being stared at so intently, continued throughout the night. Prescott's second thoughts on having given up the Alsacia were compounded when twice he had to stumble along unlighted corridors to find the open-air *letrina* in the courtyard.

Nevertheless, the Sturdevants finally had a child to call their own, and next morning, in an effort to speed up the paperwork, Prescott offered his and Sally's matching *Patek Philippes* to the dour Honduran officials. This gesture served to energize the men somewhat, but it was Mother Superior's suggestion that Sally throw in grandmother Madeleine's sapphire earrings that clinched the deal. That evening the Sturdevants were quickly escorted through customs at Toncontin and boarded one of LACSA's direct flights to LAX with brief refueling stops at Belize, Corpus Christi, Roswell and Yuma.

What an incredibly beguiling and precocious child Madeleine proved to be! She read her first story book, *My Pal, the Hunchback,* at age four, began sketching charcoals of playmates and teachers at age five, insisted on picking out her own clothes and packing her own lunch at age six and at seven, announced her determination to become a Nosecone designer at the Johnson Space Center in Houston.

As can be imagined, Baby Madeleine's prodigal bearing provoked a fair share of hostility from her classmates and teachers. Sensing that would be the case, Prescott and Sally endeavored to cushion their daughter by reassuring that she was, "Special; God's gift; superior to all other children in the Mid-Wilshire District." One might question the effect this would have on a child as she approached puberty, but for the time being, these reassurances, intended as they were, to convey unconditional love and unstinting support, succeeded beautifully.

All that changed one morning, a week before Madeleine's 8th Birthday.

"Mommy—Daddy. I need your undivided attention. I have something important to tell you."

"Can it wait until this evening, darling? Daddy and I are running late, and you're about to miss your bus."

"No, it can't. It's too important. Besides, I'm not going to school, today."

The couple exchanged alarmed looks. "Probably running a temperature," Prescott surmised as Sally placed the back of her hand on Madeleine's forehead. "Are you sick, precious? Running a fever?"

"Depends upon your definition of sick," Madeleine responded. "I think it best if you both were seated." She made this suggestion with such authority they both sat down immediately.

Madeleine began to pace, then all but spat it out, "No point in sugar-coating it. There's no way I'm going to have a rapist's baby!"

"What's that, Sugar?" Sally asked. "I don't think I heard you correctly."

"I've been raped, I'm pregnant and I need an abortion."

Prescott spat his coffee across the breakfast nook as Sally burst into gushing tears. After grabbing a wad of paper towels and sopping up the mess, Prescott demanded through clenched teeth, "What in God's name are you talking about, Madeleine?"

Between sobs, Sally begged, "Find out where she learned those awful words!"

"Which? Rapist, pregnant or abor . . . ?"

Sally cut him off. "This is no time for semantics, Prescott."

"Nor do we have time on our side," Madeleine cautioned. "The rape took place nearly eight weeks ago. I waited to see if I missed my period a second time—and I did, yesterday."

"I'm going to faint," Sally gasped and fell into a chair.

"Mommy, this isn't about you—no matter how hard you try."

Prescott pulled a bottle from the refrigerator and handed it to his wife. "Here, Sally! You know how Evian always perks you up."

After a few sips, Sally turned on him, "Prescott Sturdevant! What have you been teaching this child?"

"I might ask you the same question, Sally. What the hell do I know about missing periods?"

"Drama queens! The both of you!" Madeleine declared. "Like I said, this isn't about you or Daddy. It's about whether you want your about-to-be eight-year-old giving birth to a bastard." She paused to let this sink in. "From your silence, I'm guessing not. Everyone agrees I have a brilliant life ahead of me and I don't want it ruined by having to raise a baby not of my choosing."

"Since I didn't faint, I'll scream?" Sally announced, which she did, bloodcurdlingly. Prescott was grateful for the double-paned windows they'd recently installed as part of their upgraded solar energy package.

"What makes you . . . so sure you're . . . pregnant?" Prescott struggled to string the words together.

"What a stupid question, Press," Sally snapped. "Don't just stand there. Call the police!"

"Not your wisest move, Mommy," Madeleine cautioned. "Think how this will look to the neighbors?"

"What monster could do such a thing?" Prescott gestured to the heavens.

"I'm not prepared to reveal his identity just yet," Madeleine stated, with finality. "Priorities, Daddy. Priorities! First we locate a licensed abortionist. Then we can talk about summoning the police."

"I don't think there is such a thing as a licensed . . ." his voice faded as a tremor seized his jaw.

"It's just not possible," Sally declared. "Eight-year-olds don't have periods, and certainly aren't . . . certainly aren't . . . capable of . . ."

" . . . getting pregnant?" Madeleine finished it. "You two have led such sheltered lives."

"I have no idea where you're going with that, young lady, nor am I going to listen to another bit of hearsay or conjecture." He turned to Sally. "First, we're both calling in sick, then we're calling Wilhelm, informing him we have an emergency and demand that he see us immediately."

"Are you sure Dr. Farnsworthy is the right man?" Sally pleaded. "He's such a blabber-mouth. Remember that interview he gave the *Beverly Hills Weekly,* after he removed your Mother's vaginal polyps?"

"More to the point, if it's a true emergency, won't Dr. Farnsworthy insist you take me to the ER at Midway?" Madeleine countered in her remarkably calm voice.

"Point taken," Prescott shrugged.

With that, a Cadillac Escalade pulled into the driveway and parked directly behind Prescott's Mercedes SUV and Sally's BMW X5.

"Oh, my God!" Sally exclaimed. "The one day Emalina picks to be early. She never gets here before 10:00."

"Not a word. It's none of her business," Prescott ordered.

"With all of us still at home, she'll figure something's up," Madeleine pointed out.

"Second point taken," Prescott repeated to himself.

"If she knew about orphanages," Madeleine continued, "she'll certainly know about abortionists."

"I can't believe what I'm hearing!" It was Sally's turn to look heavenward. "What has come over my precious angel?"

"Wrong adverb, Mommy. I think you mean *into.*"

"Aaaah!" Sally cried out, and bit her knuckle just as Emalina strode through the kitchen door, carrying two small duffle bags which she surreptitiously tossed into the laundry room. *'Que pasa? Se olvidar de preparar sus relojes delante?"* ("What's happening? Forget to set your clocks ahead?")

"If that was only the problem, Emalina." Prescott moaned.

"Bien, ¿consigo un abrazo de mi genio favorito, o qué?" ("Well, can I get a hug from my favorite genius, or what?") Emalina held her arms wide. Madeleine ran to her and snuggled against her ample bosom.

"Thank God you're here," Madeleine cried out.

"Goes for all of us," Sally whispered.

"Indeed," Prescott added, vacantly.

"Why you not at school?" Emalina asked and turned to Sally, "Why you not at work?" When no answer was forthcoming, "Why your faces so long?"

"You want to tell her?" Sally gestured to Prescott.

"Not until we have it confirmed," he replied.

"Such wussies!" Madeleine snapped. "It's high time you behaved like the responsible adults you purport to be. Emalina's a grown-up. She can handle the situation—probably better than either of you."

"The 'situation,' as you call it, doesn't give you the right to sass your parents, young lady," Prescott thundered.

"Did I do something bad?" Emalina asked, fearfully. "If I did, I didn't mean to, I swear!"

"Depends on what's in the duffle bags." Madeleine couldn't resist a little taunting.

"Just some rags for the cleaning," Emalina answered, obviously uncomfortable. "And a couple of my husband's T-shirts—a few socks and underwear. I'll pay for the soap."

"We don't care about that, Emalina," Prescott affirmed.

"You've done nothing wrong," Sally assured her. "Madeleine has just handed us some distressing news."

"But before we pass it on, we have to swear you to secrecy," Prescott intoned.

A look of relief crossed Emalina's brow. "So what's a matter? Not brush her hair enough? She tear her uniform at recess?"

"How we wish," sighed Sally.

Emalina held Madeleine at arm's length and stared into her eyes. Slowly, her look of relief transmogrified into one of horror. *"Mary sagrada, mamá de Dios,"* ("Holy Mary, Mother of God,") she cried out. *"Es la sangre sobre sus calzón!"* ("It's the blood on your panties!") She reached to slap the child on the face but stopped short. Her look of horror dissolved to one of ecstasy. *"Es un milagro! Es un milagro!"* ("It's a miracle! It's a miracle!") *"¡Solamente Dios podía haber hecho tal cosa!"* ("Only God could have done such a thing!") With that, she fainted dead away.

Following her parent's manner, Madeleine looked heavenward. "So Catholic! Now, she'll never admit to knowing an abortionist."

Emalina remained comatose for several minutes while Prescott and Sally attempted to bring her around. "Put this cold towel on her forehead," he commanded. Hold her head up. Give her some of your Evian, Sally. Get her to swallow some Evian."

"She'll remember an abortionist after I reveal who the rapist is," Madeleine murmured to herself from the breakfast nook."

Emalina choked and finally blinked her eyes open, murmuring, *"Es un milagro! Es un milagro!"*

Once it was determined that Emalina was stable, Prescott resumed his campaign that Dr. Farnsworthy was the most qualified specialist for this delicate matter, and despite Emalina's protestation that, "God's will is not to be messed with," he placed the call. As luck would have it, the doctor's voicemail was filled with a flood of messages left over from the weekend by his habitual high-maintenance patients.

"Damn and double-damn!" Prescott cursed as he slammed the receiver down. "Can't even leave a goddam message!"

"El Dios está enviando un mensaje," Emalina whispered, ominously. ("God is sending a message.")

"I doubt that," Prescott snapped. "I just remembered— Farnsworthy is closed Mondays. Probably teed off at Bel Air, already."

"Por favor, Senor Prescott! I call Father Angel. He know what to do. "

"Who the hell is Father Angel?" Prescott demanded.

"Sacrilegio, Senor! Sacrilegio! He my priest. We need Father Angel's blessing, *muy pronto!*"

"Just what we *don't* need," Madeleine shouted. "Another pedophile priest—sure to deny an abortion for an eight-year-old rape victim."

"The more I hear, the more I think we need an exorcist," Sally gasped. "Do you know if Father Angel does exorcisms?"

"Stop right there, Mommy! Daddy! You too, Emalina. I'm not seeing a priest. I don't need an exorcism or his blessing. I'm not having a baby sired by a rapist nor am I having one by immaculate conception!" She glared at the three of them, then pointed to her parents. "Please, you two. I need to speak to Emalina in private."

"Where would you have us go, young lady?" The heartbreak in Sally's voice was . . . there was no other word for it . . . heartbreaking.

"I don't care, just out of earshot." She gestured to the Dutch door leading to the driveway. "Sit in your cars. Drink your coffee. This won't take long. I'll signal you when we're through."

"Alright," Prescott shrugged. "We'll be right outside. Don't try any funny business, like trying to make a run for your grandmother's house."

"Don't let her talk you into any funny business, Emalina," Sally seconded.

"You've got five minutes," Prescott warned.

"I need ten," Madeleine countered.

Prescott glanced at his Cartier. "We'll give you eight, and not a minute more," he conceded and pointedly left the door ajar.

Before she could say anything of consequence, Madeleine sensed her parents were peering through the kitchen window, trying to read her lips. Furious, she stuck her tongue out at them and ordered Emalina to close the blinds. That done, she said, "This shouldn't come as news to you, Emalina. Luisito is my rapist!"

"What you say? My boy is only twelve! Impossible! Why you say such a things? If hes Father hear this, he will kill hem for chure. This baby is a miracle, and you must leave it at that. After all I have done for you! If it wasn't for me, you would still be sleeping in that orphanage in Tegucigalpa!"

Madeleine took but a moment. "All that is true and quite beside the point. I will agree to keep Luisito's name out of it—only if you find me an abortionist. Otherwise, I tell the world. Then, I become a marvel of modern obstetrics and have an abortion, anyway. Several lives will be ruined. *Maybe even see jail time.* Do I make myself clear? It's your choice, Emalina."

Though she knew nothing of Chess, Emalina knew a checkmate when she saw it. "You must give me until tomorrow. Please, Senorita Madeleine?" she pleaded, copious tears flowing. "I cannot call heme on the phun. This personna lives in La Mir . . ." she caught herself. "This personna lives far from here. I cannot take de Escalade—my husband will see the mileage. I must take de bus."

"Heme? You said heme? The abortionist is a man? I'd prefer a woman."

"Heme *is* a senora, Senorita. Now, I'm in beeg *afligar.*"

"It's alright, Emalina. You're doing the right thing. You need some money?"

Emalina nodded, her jaw trembling.

"Daddy just gave me my allowance. I'll hide a twenty in the Downy box."

Gesturing toward the driveway, Emalina asked, "What do we tell them?"

"That you've convinced me to change my mind. That I've agreed to speak with your priest, just as soon as you can make an appointment with him."

"*Bueno. Es ta bien, Senorita.*" Emalina drew a deep breath and dabbed her eyes with a dish towel. "Don't forget veinte dineros for de bus."

Madeleine shrugged. "Right away. Now, open the blinds and tell them they can come back in."

Prescott and Sally leapt from the SUV and rushed through the door. "I can't imagine what's left for you two to be so darned secretive about," Sally complained through clenched teeth.

Madeleine attempted to convey the new story with a straight face, but eventually resorted to feigning her Mother's tearful style to hide her real feelings. Sally and Prescott surrounded and embraced her, expressing their relief with cautious enthusiasm.

Soon after, Emalina left the house, having been assured the Sturdevandts could fend for themselves, dust, vacuum and laundry-wise, at least for the time being. Within the hour, she was granted admittance to Father Angel's ECB (Emergency Confessional Booth) and conveyed the fantastic story in a staccato, rambling outburst.

Offering none of the expected pastoral commiserations, Father Angel's first question to Emalina was, "What's the family's faith?"

Her response, "Episcopal, *pienso,*" elicited a palpable sigh of relief from him, followed immediately by one of regret for the potential missed opportunity. The chance for his diocese to enrich its treasury with media money in exchange for regular 'insider' updates concerning the progress of the Miracle-Mother-to-be would be going to the Episcopalians, long regarded by the Vatican as Press-Whores. Father Angel's disappointment was tempered by the hunch that this pregnancy, if true, had not been immaculately seeded. "Let those money-grubbing Episcopalians deal with that firestorm when it comes, and come it surely will," he thought.

"Was your son intimate with this . . . Episcopalian?"

"What you mean, Father?"

"Mothers always know these things. I'm asking you, did Luisito screw this girl?"

"Father!" Emalina gasped. I never hear that word from a priest before."

"Horsefeathers!" he snapped. "My parishioners use it all the time—and much worse! I use it myself—every time I open the Cal Edison bill. Now, don't try to change the subject. Did your boy bang her?"

Emalina choked on her answer. "I don't think so. I think he's, he's . . ." she began to sob. "Pienso que es un maricone," ("I think he's gay.")

"Pray God, you're right. How soon can you get Luisito in here?"

"Luisito? Here? En el catedral? Porque, Padre? Porque?"

"We have to give him the test."

"Test? What kind of test?"

"Same one we give all adolescents contemplating the priesthood. Now, we're wasting valuable time, Senora Casañas. I want you back here with your son in an hour."

"Mio madre! I have to take heem out of school."

"One hour!"

"If you inseest. Mio madre!" she sobbed as she departed the ECB—tears being the emblematic response from just about everyone on experiencing Father Angel's cutting-edge approach.

To cover all his bases and fend off the possibility of further scandal, Father Angel rushed to his office and called the Right Reverend, Father Beverly Crest, Bishop of the Affluent Western Regions. Within moments of having the situation explained to him, Bishop Crest asked, "Has a pregnancy test been given? Can we get DNA samples from the couple without alarming anyone?"

"I didn't ask those questions," he responded meekly, "Should I have?"

"Really, Father! How else do you think we could project a budget for promoting this event as a Catholic miracle without those answers?" The Bishop sighed and went on, "I'm not ready to hand over these spoils to the Episcopalians without a fight! And, frankly I'm surprised and not a little disappointed in you. How long have you been serving Boyle Heights Parish, Father Angel?"

"Six years," he answered, clearly fearful for what might be said next.

"Perhaps the time has come for us to find you a less challenging situation." The Bishop paused to let this sink in. "I'm thinking Innercity Detroit might suit you," he added, witheringly.

"Forgive me, Father, but that doesn't seem quite fair. I called you just minutes after learning this news. I readily concede that this event might be beyond my training, but gladly re-surrender myself to be your celestial instrument—your eyes on the ground. In short, your servant."

"Everyone here at the administrative office holds special affection for you, Angel. Especially myself. Ergo, I'm liking the change of heart I'm hearing in your last sentence."

"Thank you, your Eminence, for hearing me out. Clearly I've been too quick to scoff—too cynical. Indeed, could this situation portend the second coming?"

"Unlike its transparently sound teachings on every other facet of mankind's earthly pursuits, The Holy Scriptures remain somewhat opaque on how and when God's son will reappear."

"And it's for all men of the cloth to . . ."

"Well not *all* men of the cloth," the Bishop cautioned, "but I can see you're making a sincere effort to get back on board. It's the ultimate challenge, burden, responsibility, call it what you will, for we of the Catholic priesthood to report on mankind's every transgression, judge his every accomplishment, evaluate every shred of information, no matter how lowly, so as to be totally prepared when that great Day of Salvation arrives."

"What a fool I've been! Forgive me Father. Ask anything of me. I'm all yours."

"Good to hear, my Angel. These potential miracles can all too easily slip from our grasp and be seized upon by the Evangelicals if we're not ever watchful. This young woman's situation could prove . . ."

"Forgive me, Bishop, but I have to correct you. Baby Madeleine is not a young woman—she's a child. I believe Emalina said she's about to turn eight."

"Eight, you say? If so, that further speaks to my point. Her condition could prove far more precipitous than the recent sighting of the Holy Mother's face in a Di Giorno frozen pizza, not to mention that regrettable dust-up over whether Jesus' image had actually appeared in the honey-spun yogurt vat at Dannon."

"So wise of you, Bishop Crest. You always view the broader picture."

"Thank you, Angel. Now, call me as soon as you've heard the boy's confession. Don't let him out of your ECB until you've gotten a DNA sample—a communion wafer fashioned of cardboard will do the trick—he'll never notice the difference. Then tell him you've made a mistake and have him spit it out. Finally, confirm that he's either a burgeoning breeder, a candidate for the priesthood or a Flamer. With any luck, it's the latter two."

"That's exactly what I expressed to his Mother."

"Good to see we're on the same page. Now, I must ring off. I'm late for a stockholder's meeting at Di Giorno."

As ordered, Luisito was delivered to Father Angel's ECB and detained for more than two hours while having his confession deposed.

"Papa said it was time I proved I wasn't no Maricone. Time to prove I was a man. Papa gave me some rum and told me to go find a girl and share it with her. 'Get her drunk and stick it in her,' he said. 'She'll like it, you'll like it and even if you don't your Mommy and I can stop worrying.' The only girl I know is Baby Madeleine 'cause she shares stuff—lets me play with her dolls, brush her hair, polish her nails and stuff. One day, after school, while Mommy was off shopping for Madeleine's Mommy, we drank some of that rum and played doctor and patient.

Right away, Madeleine said let's pretend my pájaro was a thermometer and I should take her temperature. Like Papa said, it felt good but it also felt funny and I said I didn't think we should do it any more. Madeleine said, "That's not fair, Luisito. You took my temperature but I didn't get to take yours." Then Mommy came back and she smelled the rum and got mad and right away drove me home. Next thing I know, Madeleine wasn't talking to me no more and Mommy said I had to come see you."

"Luisito, this must go no further than this booth," Father Angel admonished. "I am offering you an interregnum communion—without the wine, until I can get to the real thing. Put this wafer in your mouth, but don't swallow it. Understand?"

Terrified, Luisito did as bidden. Along with the threat of eternal damnation, should he reveal any part of what was said, to anyone at any time, including his parents, Father Angel gave him $200 cash to purchase condoms for use until he reached the age of consent. After that, he had to agree never to use them again without Papal dispensation.

Armed with the DNA results and other dubious evidence, Bishop Crest instigated a flurry of phone calls, first to his inside man at the Vatican, then to Mother August Angelica at the *Nuestra Madre* in Tegucigalpa. This he followed with an arm-twisting appeal to Dr. Farnsworth while riding around the Bel Air Golf Course in the Bishop's own bullet-proof cart. Finally, in a conference call between Sally, Prescott, Emalina, Father Angel and himself, he decreed that nothing short of a Mini-Ecumenical Summit could satisfy everyone's concerns.

And so, the MES was convened, for security reasons, in a private function room at *Hamburger Heaven* in Westwood. In attendance were the Sturdevants, Emalina Casañas (without her husband), Dr. Wilhelm Farnsworthy, Bishop Beverly Crest, Jimmy Chai, Crest's 18 year old 'nephew', ostensibly there to operate a tape recorder and a very insecure Father Angel. Conspicuously absent was anyone from the Episcopal Ministry and the two principals, which everyone thought apt, except Baby Madeleine, who had eavesdropped on their conference call, then pretended like she hadn't.

Prescott later commented that the mistrust in the room was so thick, you couldn't cut it with one of the Heaven's steak knives. The wariness worsened when, after introducing everyone, Bishop Crest brought up the delicate matter of who was going to pick up the lunch tab. Given the explosive nature of the situation, The Diocese could ill-afford to have its imprimatur appear on anything traceable. After some haggling, it was decided that Dr. Farnsworthy would use his

Platinum Visa, since the conference was essentially about medical research. Being a principal in a multi-practice consortium, he could turn in the receipt to Blue Cross and Medicare as legitimate expense, with little concern for an audit. Once the tab issue was off the table, a great many decisions were quickly arrived at and their public explanations carefully drilled.

It was some time after when bits and pieces of what had transpired behind those closed doors began to leak—whether by Papal edict or embittered whistle-blower, we may never know. Father Angel had a hunch that Jimmy Chai was the logical snitch, particularly after Bishop Crest hobbled into a Chastity Seminar sporting a black eye and a sprained wrist and made no effort to explain his condition.

Eventually an audio tape, allegedly from the Hamburger Summit, surfaced at CNN's Hollywood NewsDesk, but after careful reviewing, the producers agreed, rather than risk incurring the Vatican's wrath, it would be best to respect everyone's privacy and let sleeping babies lie. Nancy Grace was furious with their decision, but more on her, later.

What follows are excerpts from that poorly recorded tape:

Dr. Farnsworth: (Apparently rehearsing what he would explain to Baby Madeleine in his follow-up consultation.) "Preliminary test indicate it's a (inaudible). It's of some size, to be sure, but essentially (inaudible). We're monitoring it closely, Baby (inaudible), but at this point we don't think it advisable to (inaudible) until it has become fully (inaudible). In the meantime, (inaudible) Madeleine you may continue your daily (inaudible) much as you did before the (inaudible)."

Prescott: (Drilling the explanation he was instructed to give his mother and mother-in-law.) "Madeleine has been told she's developed a rare (inaudible). While benign, it's a (inaudible) tumor that can't be operated on until it's fully (inaudible). Our trusted (inaudible) Emalina and her priest,

Father (inaudible) have suggested that we should fly Baby Madeleine back to (inaudible) for the operation, a country well known for its (inaudible) specialists. Sally and Madeleine have agreed, and now that *Sally is pregnant*, and it looks like she'll be at full term at the same time Madeleine's tumor (inaudible), both have chosen to recuperate under the care of the Maccabee (inaudible) at the (inaudible) where we found Madeleine in the first place. God willing, when this is all over, you'll both have a second (inaudible) to dote on."

In the background, one could clearly hear an unidentified male voice making a derisive comment about it being "One helluva' story to keep straight." Perhaps it was the mysterious Jimmy Chai?

Bishop Crest is heard composing a bulletin he hoped the Vatican would approve to be telexed across Mexico and Latin America. Apparently he was seated closer to the microphone, as his words are crystal clear: "For Immediate Release: We have received credible information that Jesus, the Son of God may be returning soon. As before, he will appear in the form of a humble, immaculately conceived baby boy. A bright star will hang low to mark his birthplace—which could be anywhere from El Paso, Texas to all of Mexico and the Isthmus of Panama, possibly even the interiors of Colombia or Venezuela. We're asking all true Christians in those areas to remain on high alert and for every devout Catholic to dig deep into their tithing pockets so that we may welcome Our Savior, Lord Jesus, the Son of God in the style to which he has been denied for nearly 2000 years."

It was only after pirated dupes of this tape were circulated that any real sense could be made of what happened. Mother August, seeing a chance for a buck, leapt at the plan: If it was a boy, the orphanage would keep it. Then, after surreptitiously distributing photographs of Madeleine's swollen belly as authentication, the boy-child could easily be promoted as the reincarnated Baby Jesus. When that hypothesis wore thin, the boy could learn journeyman carpentry and help maintain the ever expanding orphanage. At all costs, he must never be raised in the Episcopal religion!

If it was a girl, the Sturdevants were welcome to take her home. She would provide them with a much desired 2nd child—Madeleine would no longer be 'Baby Madeleine,' and it would give her someone closer to her size to pick on.

Garth Sparkle, Sally's hair colorist, had a girlfriend named Spade who worked in prosthetics at Universal Studios. After hearing Sally's story and being sworn to secrecy, Spade kindly arranged for her to rent a series of ultra-realistic pregnancy appliances sculpted in graduating sizes.

Things didn't progress so smoothly for Baby Madeleine, however. At six months, despite her baggy shirts and elasticized running pants, she could no longer hide her 'tumor' and became acutely embarrassed at recess. With the first sign of morning sickness, after she threw up her breakfast, she seemed to loose a good part of her sass. On a more positive note, it was the onset of morning sickness that triggered the beginning of Mother and daughter's serious re-bonding.

"I just hope my baby doesn't come the same time they have to operate on your tumor," Sally said, meaning just the opposite.

Madeleine played right along with the ruse. "I hope you have a girl, Mommy. I need someone to practice Veterinary with. I already played human doctor with Luisito and look what that got me!"

The Baby Madeleine story would have a near-perfect ending were it not for the relentless pecking of certain NewsHens. As planned, during their eighth month, Madeleine and Sally checked into Hospital San Felipe, which despite its enormous size, appeared to be extremely well run. A first-rate team of doctors, including a pair of obstetric surgeons from Costa Rica and Miami, were flown in on Bishop Crest's dime to oversee this extraordinary event.

On the fateful day, Sally and Madeleine were placed on adjoining tables, with only a curtain separating them. Naturally, Madeleine was heavily sedated, while her Mother insisted on 'not wanting to miss anything' and delivering 'wide awake.' When the big moment finally arrived, despite having attended numerous Lamaze classes, Prescott was too nervous to be of any use to either his wife or his daughter and chose to pace the waiting room with Bishop Crest.

Miraculously, Sally's water broke (in reality, she spilled a bottle of Evian) at the exact moment the surgeons successfully relieved Madeleine of her tumor by Caesarian section. To the astonishment and delight of everyone in the delivery room, the tumor proved to be a perfectly formed baby girl, weighing in at 6 ½ pounds. After cutting the cord and wiping off the gorgeous creature, it was brought 'round to Sally and placed between her legs.

"Empujar! Empujar!" her nurses shouted, having been carefully rehearsed, though the level of zeal in their voices was not what one would expect—the devout among them having prayed for a Baby Jesus. Sally immediately commenced to count contractions between her screams, making certain they were loud enough to be heard from the waiting room.

Exhausted, she could not hold back tears of relief and joy when the nurses placed the newborn brunette in her arms. Immediately, Prescott was escorted into the room by the head nurse. Bishop Crest was trailed by Mother August Angelica, struggling not to look downcast.

Prescott kissed Sally on the forehead. "She has your eyes, he said.

"And your mouth," Sally said to him.

"And Luisito's everything else, I'll bet," said Madeleine groggily, from behind the curtain.

"Sorry things didn't work out quite as we'd hoped," said the Bishop, offering his hand, "but no hard feelings."

"You're sorry! I'll tell you who's sorry!" snorted Mother August.

"We are eternally grateful for your help, Bishop. If Sally and I can ever return the favor, don't hesitate to ask."

"Thank you, Press, but that's not necessary. I think we'll just keep this thing as our little *Ecumenical* secret," he winked.

Out in the waiting room, a TV mounted high on the wall, blinked on.

"Good evening. Welcome to CNN World News Update. This just in: Our Honduran affiliate in Tegucigalpa is reporting that an unidentified 8 year old American girl has just given birth to a 6 ½ pound baby. Early reports tell us both mother and child are healthy and recovering nicely. That's all we have for now, but rest assured, we're on this, like flies on cow pies. We'll be giving you further updates as soon as our correspondent locates a working pay phone. Now, back to Anderson Cooper and 360."

"Thanks, Campbell. My people are on top of this riveting story as well. I'm speaking to you from the Big Island of Hawaii, where behind me, lava from Mt. Kilauea's latest eruption is flowing right to the edge of Waimeatown and threatens to wipe out the second largest cattle ranch in the world. I'll be leaving the Island right after this edition of '360' to fly directly to Honduras. With God on our side, I and my crew should be landing in Tegucigalpa first thing in the morning."

The image switched to Nancy Grace standing on an expansive front lawn flooded in bright light. Underneath, the Chyron whizzed by: "Underage Birth Shocks Upscale Hancock Park Neighborhood!"

"I'll take it from here, Anderson," Grace smiled. "That's the Prescott Sturdevant residence directly behind me. We've traced the plates on the Escalade parked in the driveway to an Escamilyo Casañas, whose wife, Emalina, appears to be hold up inside. It's not yet been established what Mrs. Casañas' relationship to the Sturdevants is, but authorities fear—and how many times have we seen this before?—authorities fear this could quickly escalate into a hostage situation. Unfortunately, the neighbors have refused to cooperate and will not answer any of our questions on background. But we're going to hang out here all night, if we have to. Back to you, Campbell."

Lisa In Black

Tuesday morning, 6:40 am at LAX and block-long lines zigzagged from inside to outside the terminal, crowding the sidewalk. Since 9/11, the horror stories about intensified security measures had grown exponentially and here again was living proof, as if any of us needed it.

My driver waited while I struggled to insert three wilted bills into the rack and yanked a reluctant cart from its ranks. He stacked my bags on it, wished me a safe trip and drove off into the phosphorescent smog. I bumped my way past the hordes hoping to check in at curbside and edged myself into the e-Ticket queue awaiting boarding passes at the United counter inside the terminal.

Some distance ahead of me, looking like Martha Graham exhumed, a woman somewhere in her late 60's, possibly early 70's, shuffled, crane-like, through the maze. As the line advanced, it periodically brought us abreast of each other and I could see she was dressed entirely in black. Having achieved the look of the defiantly eccentric, I got the idea she was straining to be noticed while pretending not to be. Several folks around me made an effort not to stare as they whispered commentary to themselves and each other.

'Bizarre' couldn't begin to describe the black skullcap supporting what appeared to be an African dildo sprouting from the top of her head, with three shiny-blonde bagel-shaped chignons coiled around it. This exotic headpiece, along with six-inch platform heels concealed under a floor-length skirt, made her appear seven feet tall. A fake-fur rug was folded over her left arm and she clutched a Naugahyde weekender bag with her left hand. To complete the image, with her right hand, she dragged an outsized black suitcase secured with a bit of clothesline painted Chinese red, the only splash of color in her ensemble.

Our next close encounter revealed a five-inch-wide vinyl belt cinching her waist, with a huge buckle clasped just below her non-existent bosom. Each surreptitious glance revealed another weird component: bronzing cream streaked her face like Watusi war paint; ebony lipstick the texture of Velcro matched her noir-polished nails. Something about the drape of her skirt shouted 'homemade' yet no part of her looked to have been laundered in a very long time. I couldn't help recalling a friend's rejoinder when confronted with excessive fashion: "My dear, go back in the house, take off any three things and you'll still be overdressed."

Still, I couldn't take my eyes off her. Nor, could anyone else. Something about her over-the-shoulder, cockatoo-like glance was ringing my memory bell when the woman behind me whispered to her companion, "Is that the perfect outfit for a plane ride or what?" Someone else grumbled, "Must be a Drag Queen." "Obviously a blind one," hissed another. "Maybe she's in mourning?" a fourth voice wondered in a sympathetic tone. "No, that's definitely a real woman," I chimed in, though unsure what had given me such conviction.

When, finally, The Lady in Black approached the counter, she towered over the tiny, round female agent, who exuded that she'd seen it all before and would tolerate no nonsense from the creature staring down at her imperiously.

"Trust me, Honey, they're not gonna' let you carry all that stuff on board," she declared. "Way too big. And way too heavy, Darlin'. Best you take it up with my Supervisor. He's the good lookin' gentleman in the blue jacket at the other end of the counter. He can hardly wait to help you, Sweetheart."

The din of the crowd drowned out Lady In Black's response, though her body language spoke volumes. With a gesture purloined from the *Wicked Witch of The West*, she pointed a gnarled finger at the Supervisor, indicating he should come to her, which he deftly ignored. Clearly, some long-established code between ticket-agent and Supervisor had been established, for zaftig lady nodded and called out, "Next in line!" A neatly-dressed family of four rushed forward.

"Mommy, is that the lady from *Harry Potter*?" their eight-year-old boy asked, in a piping voice.

"She's scaring me," whimpered their six-year-old girl. Grinning sheepishly, Mommy and Daddy leaned to shush them, providing a heartwarming *Kodak Moment* for the rest of us.

Furious, The Lady in Black shifted into giraffe-gait in preparation for descending on the Supervisor. Before she reached him, a space at the opposite end of the counter opened up for me and I lost sight of her, though I hoped we might catch up at the security gates.

I resisted offering snarky responses to the questions, 'Did you pack your own bags? Have they been in your possession at all times? Has anyone asked you to carry anything on board for them?' and concentrated on getting my seat assignment moved as far forward as possible. Claustrophobia, especially on airplanes, is a serious issue for me.

Suddenly there was a terrific commotion at the other end of the hall. Drug-sniffing dogs appeared, whining and barking at full decible. Their DEA handlers ordered the crowd to stand back and stay calm. At the center of the melee, The Lady in Black leaned against a pillar, her Afro-phallic headpiece giddily askew, keening at a pitch that would have done a Patmos funeral proud.

"Good God!" I thought. "Is it possible she's a drug mule?"

The woman standing directly behind me whacked her husband on the shoulder and seconded my thought. "I told you she was a drug dealer, Morty! Didn't I? Not five minutes ago. Didn't I? Who else would wear an outfit like that?"

Similar comments rippled through the anxious crowd: "Not necessarily. Drug dealers look like anybody, these days.'

"Watch *Entertainment Tonight*. They'll tell you."

"Maybe she's got a bomb hidden in that topknot?"

"Or in her platform shoes."

"If nothing else, she's a walking crime of fashion."

"I'm surprised the cops haven't already given her a ticket for that outfit."

Lastly, and nearly in chorus, "Long as they don't let her on *our flight*."

By the time my bags were checked, I was handed my boarding pass and started for the security gates, the DEA guys, their dogs and the Lady in Black had vanished without a trace. Or so it seemed until something on the floor caught my eye. It resembled a large beetle so I bent down to get a closer look. 'Dead beetles laying around LAX? Impossible,' I assured myself, but curiosity triumphed. First determining that nobody was watching, I picked up the curved object. Black and rough on one side, pink and smooth on the other—I realized it was a fake fingernail! Of course! The Lady In Black must have lost it in her struggle with the DEA! I slipped it into my pocket and hoped, for her sake, it hadn't been glued on too firmly.

After flashing my Pacemaker ID, I was directed around the metal detector and given a thorough pat down by a sinister-looking man with breath so toxic it would have singed my beard, had I not shaved earlier. Satisfied that I was not secreting explosives under my scrotum or in my anal passage, he signaled the okay to retrieve my carryon bag which had passed through the x-ray machine without incident.

This was amazing since I had packed it so hastily that morning. It contained a stopwatch, rubbing alcohol, toenail and fingernail clippers, a disposable razor, a metal comb, a pair of pinking shears, two bungi cords, a teakwood letter opener, 2 triple AAA batteries and a souvenir candle from a friend's birthday party. What the hell was I thinking of? For a brief moment, I contemplated turning myself in, but fear that Halitosis Harry had relatives working the Interrogation Section, stopped me.

With no further sign of the Lady in Black, I found myself concerned for her, wondering what provoked the ominous appearance of the DEA dogs and their Nordic handlers. A pang of envy engulfed me when I imagined her being body searched by the Olympiads.

Meticulously trained in calming techniques and diplomatic evasiveness, none of the personnel at the gate admitted to having any information about the DEA incident. "Please have your boarding passes, along with your picture I.D. out and ready when you approach the jetway. We'll be boarding momentarily, starting with the rear of the aircraft. Thank you for your cooperation and welcome aboard United flight #102, non-stop to New York."

Dozing on the long flight, it came to me in a dream who the Lady In Black must be! No wonder she looked familiar! Jesus! Was my memory that bad? I sat up, signaled for a cup of water and reached into my pocket for a tissue but produced the fake finger-nail instead. Over an inch long, covered with textured black enamel, it looked to be intentionally sinister. And then it hit me like a thunderbolt. Despite all the years that had passed, all the blood under the bridge, the severing of all communication, how could I have forgotten?

Lisa Fontaine was her stage name. How many decades ago? I winced to think about it. We were teenagers then, at least I was, thrilled to be part of a gaggle of stage-struck hopefuls working in a former auto repair shop on the Jersey shore tricked out as a summer stock theatre. Despite being located three long blocks from the ocean, it was named "The Surfside" and that's where I learned to spell theatre with an 're' in order to distinguish it from its proletariat stepsister, the movie theater. It wasn't until the second season when I realized how pretentious it had been to call that oil-soaked garage a theater—by any spelling.

We rehearsed around the clock to perform a new musical revue each Wednesday through Sunday nights, along with an extemporized children's play on Wednesday and Thursday matinees. Opening two new shows on the same day nearly killed us, but we were young, wildly enthusiastic and thrilled to be working in "the theatuh." We endured these rigors from mid-June to Labor Day in exchange for room and board at a cottage coyly named "Offstage" and five dollars a week. I was given an extra fiver because I built the meager sets, ran the dimmer boards and painted signs and posters in addition to occasionally appearing onstage.

My first impression of Lisa was how skinny she was, and how awkward her stage movements, despite her claims of having studied under Agnes deMille and Jack Cole. The thinness of her voice was particularly disconcerting, given that almost every show was a musical. Lisa seemed to be on the defensive from the outset, but it wasn't long before I saw how her drive and determination might offset her technical deficiencies. As the season progressed, our season subscribers, who always sat in the front row, appeared willing to ignore her wavering pitch, shortness of breath and unsteady rhythm, and allowed that Lisa's voice was 'interesting'.

One weekend in late July, Mabel, Lisa's mother, bussed down from New York to visit her and check out the theatre. Mabel took a shine to me and invited me to join them for lunch in the local Drug Store (Dutch, of course). Over a twenty-cent chicken salad sandwich and a five cent Coke, I accidentally learned Lisa's real name and how smart she had been to change it. The family name was 'Funk or Fluck or Farhtz, or something real close, so help me! I remember wondering how a man with such an unfortunate name had talked Lisa's shy, retiring mother into marrying him, though, by the time I met Mabel Farhtz, (Funk? Fluck?) she'd long been separated or divorced. It was not clear which.

Not five minutes into that meal, Mabel set decorum aside to rail on about, "That no good, worthless S.O.B! Such a tightwad! Morris left us without a pot to piss in. Didn't even bother to say goodbye, can you imagine? And mean! Nobody meaner in all of New York than Morris Farhtz, let me tell you!" She looked around to see if she was being overheard. "But nobody gets away with being mean to my Mavis anymore, do they, Honey?"

"It's Lisa, Mother. How many times do I have to tell you?" she hissed. "I'm Lisa Fontanne. Nobody in show business knows me as Mavis Fahrtz and nobody is going to, if I can help it." She glared at me, determined to blockade any further discussion.

Later in the season, when we had time to sit around placing cashless wagers on who among us had the best chance to *make it on Broadway*, several of us wondered why Mr. Hayden, our chubby, forty-something leprechaun of a producer, had picked Lisa in the first place.

Joe, as he insisted we call him in that disingenuously democratized, "I'm just one of you," style that none of us bought for a minute, was notorious for the cattle calls he staged at Variety Arts Studios in Manhattan every Spring. From the army of hopefuls he picked his 'stars of tomorrow,' as he frequently addressed us, though I, being the only 'technical type,' didn't quite fit that gratuitous soubriquet. In addition to his talent for spotting tomorrow's stars who would work for a pittance today, Mr. Hayden had an eye for pre-pubescent boys. Fortunately, his strict Catholic upbringing kept that dangerous penchant in check, having in all probability, fostered it in the first place.

By August, gossip about his playing games with the neighbor's nine-year-old—just the two of them—for hours on end, had reached a threatening pitch, provoking Joe to call the company together in the communal living room. He delivered a gut-wrenching denial about "Not being one of those perverts, despite the nasty rumors certain members of this company have been circulating about me. If they continue, all responsible parties will be fired immediately. I mean business, so don't test me." This last was choked out through crocodile tears that moved no one in the room but himself. Even at seventeen, I could sense the man was torn with guilt and in deep denial.

As the season wore on, Lisa was given fewer and fewer solos. She began to complain, at first just to herself in a mumbling scold, but soon she was hectoring anyone who would listen, and there weren't many so I became her favorite wailing wall. She went on and on about what a cheap-assed producer Joe was, how she was sick of wearing those gawd-awful tube tops, which, in purporting to fit every woman, flattered none. What she didn't say was how badly the quilted stretch fabric emphasized her flat chest. "Only a goddamned fairy would force real women to wear such an ugly thing," she snarled.

By the time this epithet had reached Joe, there was only two weeks left in the season. He must have taken pity on Lisa for he gave her the beautiful lament, "My Ship," as a solo in our tribute to "Lady In The Dark." By calling it a 'Tribute,' and not using actual dialogue from the musicals, Joe avoided having to pay royalties. This duplicitous format saved him a fortune, though we were twice visited by men in black suits, purportedly from New York, rumored to represent ASCAP and BMI. During their visits, Joe sweated profusely, popped several rolls of Tums and later claimed to have 'ironed-out any silly misunderstandings.'

Which brings me to that night in late August when, after the evening's performance, most of the company had adjourned to the nearby bowling alley to celebrate Joe's birthday. A day or two before, Lisa overheard me confessing to Frank Albany, the lead male dancer, that bowling held absolutely no interest for me. She took me aside and confessed to feeling the same, although I was about to learn, she had other forms of recreation in mind.

All summer, I had been covertly pining for Frank, the lead dancer and he'd finally agreed to meet me in the attic dorm area that night, so we could 'talk over Catholicism,' which he claimed to have carried him through rough patches growing up in an orphanage in the city from which he'd taken his name. Coincidentally, my sister was taking classes in Catholicism in preparation for marrying one and I had always been attracted to the opulent pageantry of its ceremonies. Since Frank had heretofore excelled at bowling, I hoped his willingness to meet clandestinely meant he was interested in me romantically.

After curtain calls, I handed Joe a birthday card, repeated my 'upset stomach' excuse from Boy Scout days and volunteered to stay behind to turn off the lights and lock up the theatre. I finished the tasks quickly, thumbed a ride home and jumped into the shower in preparation for my hoped-for assignation. Picturing Frank's blue eyes, shiny brunette hair and chiseled features made drying myself off somewhat awkward. When I stepped from the bathroom, wrapped only in my towel, Lisa was waiting for me, a disconcerting glint in her eye.

"Hope I didn't scare you?" she cooed.

"Well, you did," I stammered. "Jeezz, Lisa, I thought I was here all by myself. How come you're not at the party?"

"I had something I want to talk to you about. Just the two of us. Can you spare a minute? You're the only one I can trust around here," she added, petulantly.

"Well, sure, I guess. I mean, why not?" Lying always made me stutter. Shit! What was she doing here? And why was I being so damned polite? Frank could walk through the front door any minute and my whole plan would be ruined. "Let me put on my clothes," I mumbled, clutching my towel as I pushed past her and started up the stairs.

She eyed me suspiciously. "Are you expecting someone?"

"What do you mean? Jeeze, Lisa, let me get dressed, would you?" I whined as I scrambled up the steps. The last thing I wanted was her to follow me, which she promptly did, stopping at the landing.

"Don't worry. I'll wait here," she smirked. "I promise I won't watch, though, it might be fun."

"What is she up to?" I wondered. Still damp from the shower and the beginnings of panic-sweat, I struggled to pull on my socks and sneakers. "So, what is it you want to talk about, Lisa?" I called towards the stairwell.

"Relationships. I'm in the market for one. Know any likely candidates?"

My jeans felt like they were lined with glue and, in my haste, I managed to pull my T-shirt on inside out. I had to find some way to signal Frank to stay away until I could convince Lisa she belonged back at Joe's birthday party. But, by the time I reached the landing, it was too late. Frank was opening the front door.

"What brings you home so early?" Lisa asked, her eyebrows at full mast.

I could feel the blood rushing to my cheeks and on a look from Frank, started to answer for him, but he cut me off smoothly.

"Bob and I are going to have a talk about God and my church. And that's as much as you need to know, Lisa."

Wow! What a guy! With one sentence, Frank added the aphrodisiac of pride to my infatuation for him.

Lisa flinched visibly, then spun around to face me. "I thought you were an agnostic or atheist?"

"Who told you that?" Gulping a deep-breath mixture of relief and trepidation, I continued, "Religion is a private matter." Emboldened by Frank's stance, I added, "He's right. It's really none of your business, Lisa."

She looked as if she was about to slap me, then abruptly changed her mind. "Well, pardon me—big time!" She remained silent for a moment, trembling with rage, and declared, "If *nobody else* needs to shower before having a religious discussion, I'm going to use it."

Frank shrugged, as if to say, "Suit yourself,"

Shit! That meant she was probably *in for the night*. Angry but afraid to express myself, I glanced at Frank who seemed maddeningly unperturbed. Lisa climbed the stairs and sneered over her shoulder, "If it's privacy you two want, I suggest you hike yourselves up to the beach." Then, in her most sarcastic tone yet, "Better take a blanket. Beach sand can get into the damnedest places."

To my surprise, Frank said, "Good idea, let's do it."

"Alright," I agreed, a shade too enthusiastically. "There's a comforter hanging on the back clothesline. Ought to be dry by now."

"I'll help you," he replied, crinkling his eyes, guileless as to how much that turned me on.

'This might turn out alright, after all,' I assured myself, as we trudged toward the blue-white dunes shimmering in the outer-space ambience of the full moon. I stole glances at Frank, wondering which was more beautiful—the setting or him. By the time we'd picked a spot near the surf, put down the comforter and slipped out of our shoes, I knew there was no contest.

We lay side-by-side, arms folded under our heads, staring up at the diamond-strewn sky. The waves, crashing majestically at our feet, made excuse for our silence. "This is right out of the movies," I thought. Specifically, "From Here to Eternity," and wondered if I was looking as much like Deborah Kerr to Frank, as he was Burt Lancaster to me.

Finally, it was he who broke the silence. "I've never done this before," he whispered, a hint of anguish in his voice. "Never found anybody I wanted to do it with."

Blinking back tears of joy, I said "I'm flattered," and turned to put my face close to his.

"I mean it, Bob. I always thought I'd have to wait until I got married."

I was *that close* to kissing him, but something said hold back. "Married? Why would you think that?" I asked, suddenly alarmed.

"To talk in detail—about—you know, religion, God, The Mother Church. I never thought a guy, especially a non-Catholic, would be interested enough to discuss it with me."

"Oh," was all I managed.

"My wife will have to be Catholic. I decided that a long time ago. Obviously, she can't be a nun, but I hope to find a woman who has all the qualities of a nun." He turned to me, momentarily flustered by the proximity of our faces. "Wrap the comforter around you if you're that cold," he mumbled. "Here, take my share if you want."

"No, no, no. I'm alright," I lied, while trying to think what to say next.

"I want to have kids, three or four, maybe more and I'll raise them in the Catholic faith. No question about it."

"I see," was my earth-shattering reply as I retreated to my side of the comforter.

"How about you?" Frank continued. "Don't you want your wife to be a . . . you're a Methodist, right?"

There was no mistaking the quavering in my voice. "I'm not sure I'm ever going to get married, Frank," and immediately prayed the surf had drowned me out. When Frank flinched, I knew it hadn't.

"What are you saying, Bob?" He sat up, as if preparing to leap from the comforter.

Fearing the stridency in his voice, I back-peddled. "I'm saying I want a career in the theatre—I want it so bad, I'm not sure I can find a woman willing to take a back seat to my ambition. And even if I did find one, how fair would that be?" I was paraphrasing dialogue from some movie—I couldn't remember which—probably one of Bette Davis' but Frank didn't seem to notice.

"Then find a girl who's also in show-business. That ought to be easy for you." Reassured by his simple logic, he lay back down. "It's obvious, at least two chicks in the company have the hots for you. Though you don't seem to give them the time of day."

"If you're referring to Lisa, do you blame me?"

"No, I wasn't talking about Lisa. I was thinking specifically of Louise."

"Your dance partner? I thought she was after you, Frank."

"She was, at the beginning of the season, but my ballet teacher back in Poughkeepsie always said 'Never mix business with pleasure.' Louise's nice enough, just not my type. Besides, she's Baptist."

"Oh, but you think it's okay for a Baptist to marry a Methodist?" I chuckled, momentarily reprieved.

"Father McConnell says all Protestant religions are basically the same, no matter what they call themselves."

"Really. And who is Father McConnell?" Encouraged by the playfulness in Frank's voice, I leaned in close, once again, to study his beautiful lashes and lips.

"The head priest at the orphanage. I guess Father McConnell was the closest thing any of us had to a real Father. He died this past spring. I couldn't afford the trip to Schenectady for his funeral."

The catch in Frank's voice was unmistakable but I was barely listening, too busy tallying up the score of my romantic encounter to date: Driven from the house, if not by a woman scorned, one doing a darned good imitation of one; Frank had voiced his determination to find a suitable Catholic woman willing to bear a minimum of four children for him. Add in that he seemed determined to hook me up with one or more of his rejects. Finally, his veneration for a recently deceased priest had all but placed the man's body between us, at least in my frustrated mind.

With total disregard for any logical transition, I asked, as nonchalantly as I could, "You ever fooled around with another guy, Frank?"

He waited for some time before answering. "What exactly do you mean by 'fooling around'?"

Even at that tender age, I could hear an encouraging inflection where there was none. That long-ago nano-second lying on a moonlighted dune, misted by salty waves presaged a life-long pattern of daredevil persistence when smitten.

"Come on, Frank. You know what I mean—giving each other a back rub, wrestling and hugging—maybe unbuttoning our dungarees." He didn't move and continued to stare at the sky. "Give it a try, Frank. You might like it."

"I don't think you'd better say any more, Bob. I'm feeling sick to my stomach, and I *don't like that.*"

Panicked, I pleaded, "Frank, you must have figured out by now how much I like you? Why did you come here with me if you didn't?"

He paused thoughtfully. "Because you seemed like a nice guy—and smart. I like being around smart people."

"Thank you, but I'm two years younger than you. How smart can I be?"

"Doesn't matter. I know I'm not as intelligent as you so I figured I might learn something. But what you're talking about is a sin, Bob. You know darned well it is." He sighed deeply and turned to face me, tears glinting in his lashes. "Father McConnell warned us that we'd all go to hell if we so much as talked about it."

Frank's beauty and vulnerability had me stumbling for words. "Frank, I'm really sorry . . . if I upset you. That's the furthest thing . . . from my mind."

He shivered and lightly placed his palm against my chest. "It's not you, Bob, exactly. It's just that . . ." His voice trailed off though he continued to stare at me without blinking.

Confused, I had to ask, "How did the subject ever come up with your priest?"

"I don't remember. And if I did, I couldn't tell you." The slightest hint of a smile illuminated his eyes and curved his lips. "Cause you're a Methodist."

"Like that really matters, Frank. I can't help wondering how a priest could know so much about it—if he . . ."

" . . . if he didn't have first hand experience?" Frank finished the sentence. "Look, if you're trying to get me to say something bad about Father McConnell, don't."

"I won't. I promise. But it's got to make you wonder." Even forlorn, Frank looked so handsome. I was hard-pressed to conceal my arousal.

A thick cloud passed over the moon, turning the sand a charcoal gray. "We should have brought a flashlight?" I suggested, not really meaning it.

He shrugged. "Now I'm cold. If you promise to shut up for five minutes, maybe we could just hold onto each other for a little while. But no funny stuff, you promise?"

At that moment, I would have promised him anything. I mimed 'zipping' my mouth and reached to put my hand on his shoulder but Frank guided it to his fly and, after sighing again, kissed me full on the mouth. I trembled in ecstasy, hoping his kiss wasn't considered 'funny stuff.' Testing what might be, I tugged at his zipper.

"Nope. That's as far as it goes," Frank said, grabbing my hand. "We're keeping everything zipped, remember?"

He kissed me again and thrust his crotch against my hand, provoking such bliss, I was ready to ejaculate, no matter what.

"Anything more would be a sin against God," he murmured. "And I'm not ready for that."

"You're so beautiful, Frank! You take my breath away. How can anything this wonderful be a sin?"

"Just be happy with what you got. You're only the . . . second guy I ever went this far with." He stroked his hand against my zipper. "Looks like you must have done this before."

"Oh, God, Frank. Don't. I can't hold back." At once in ecstasy and mortified, I felt my crotch moistening and moved to turn away, but Frank held me tightly against him.

"It's okay, Bob. It's okay. You couldn't help it. Another minute and both of us would have been in real trouble."

"I'm all wet," I moaned. "How am I going to get back in the house? Everybody will see it."

Frank pulled me closer to him so that we fused head to toe. "Now I'm all wet, too," he winked. If ever there was a moment deserving to be frozen in time, this was it. And it was my turn to get misty-eyed as Frank allowed me to kiss him all over his face.

"Okay. That's enough, Rapid Robert." He pushed me away. "Don't want you gettin' too used to this." He leaped to his feet and executed a series of grande jeté across the sand. "Follow me, Mr. Rabbit," he commanded as he ran into the surf. "Nothing like a midnight swim to get your pants really wet!"

"Of course! Why didn't I think of that?" I dove into the waves and allowed a breaker to carry me ashore. "You're the smart one, Frank," I called out. For a moment, the undertow felt like it was about to sweep me off my feet, but Frank grabbed my arm, pulled me to him and held fast. The cloud cover moved on permitting the neon-moon to re-illuminate the expanse of dunes.

"Don't look just yet, but I think someone is watching us," he whispered.

"Where?"

"At the top of the dune."

"Who?"

"Don't know." Frank pushed me away roughly.

"What's to see? Two guys having a midnight swim?"

"Could be Louise. They say she's still carrying the torch."

"It would be something else if we were bare-assed."

"She could have been watching the whole time."

"It was pitch black until a minute ago, Frank. And we were in my comforter."

His eyes narrowed to slits. "I don't like the looks of this. Not one bit. You go on ahead. I'm gonna stay back for awhile."

"That's crazy. Arriving separately will only make us look guilty of something."

"Do as I say. And don't speak to me for the next couple of days—about anything—'til I figure this out."

"Okay. But I'll leave the comforter. You're going to need it."

"No I won't," he snapped. "You take it. Hide it under the back porch or something."

"Better I put it back on the clothesline."

That was Sunday night. If Frank ever showed up at the house, it had to have been after I collapsed in sleep. And he was nowhere to be seen next morning. Monday was supposed to be our day off—but it was also laundry day, housecleaning day—our only time to get personal stuff done. I was heartsick when I learned Frank had disappeared without a word to anyone and when he didn't return Monday night, I tossed and turned, unable to sleep—afraid to speak about my concerns to anyone, scared I'd reveal my true feelings.

Tuesday morning, as we were waiting on the van to take us to the theatre, Joe informed us that Frank had undergone emergency dental work off-island, that he would be returning to "Offstage" later in the day and would be resting thereafter. He added ominously, "It is important that he get lots of rest and no one disturbs him." The last seemed directed solely at me.

Rehearsals were excruciatingly painful and dragged on through the day and late into the evening. As it was the final show of the season, everyone was exhausted and all the dance numbers had to be restaged in case Frank was unable to perform on Wednesday. Fortunately, his role as the 'Dancing Cobbler' in the Children's matinee of *Rumpelstiltskin* could be easily cut.

I was occupied with sprucing up tired flats, stringing bug lights and ball fringe and rewiring the dry-ice fog machine in an effort to fulfill Joe's dictum about "Always end the season with a splash. Always give them something extra," he declared, but when presented with a request for a few yards of muslin or a new staple gun, he modified his maxim. "Always leave them wanting a little more." I was counting the minutes until I could get back to the house and have a word with Frank.

At 10:00 pm, when the van finally pulled up in front of 'Offstage', I was the first off it, with the excuse I needed to use the bathroom right away. I flew up the stairs, two steps at a time—my heart pounding as in a marathon and ran to the rear of the attic. When I saw that the curtain was drawn over Frank's cubicle and his reading light didn't appear to be on, I tapped on the door frame. "Frank, I know what you said about not talking and all, but I . . . everyone wants to know if you're alright."

There was no response, no sound of any kind. "Frank, please? Speak to me. Even if it's just to tell me to go away. I'll understand, but I'm worried about you. Please, Frank?" Real panic, unlike anything I'd ever experienced before, seized me. I parted the curtain gingerly and will never forget the sight that awaited me.

Dangling like a rag doll, Frank's head lolled to one side, choked by a leather belt looped through a length of clothesline he'd tied to the rafters. A café chair lay on its side, just beyond his blue-white feet.

"Oh, my God, Frank! Oh, my God! What have you done?" I called out in an anguished whisper in the hope no one but he would hear me and somehow I could repair this awful sight before anyone else saw it. I wrapped my arms around his knees and struggled to lift him up, but it was no use. What they say about a dead man's weight is true. My effort caused an awful cracking sound, either from the beam above or Frank's neck. I was reduced to wailing and sobbing like I've never experienced since.

Joe was the first to enter the tiny space. "Get away from him, Bob! Get away right now! You're only making things worse." Several cast members crowded behind him and began to cry out as they caught glimpse of the horrific sight. "I'm calling the police," Lisa yelled.

"No you're not!" Joe thundered. "I'm the one in charge here and I'm the one who will speak to the police. Is that clear? Now, everyone go to your rooms and stay calm. We'll have everything under control in a few minutes. I know this is tough, but we've got a long day ahead of us and two openings tomorrow night, so you'd best try to put this out of your heads and get some sleep. Remember, you are artists—professionals in the theatre where the show *always goes on*, no matter what!"

Grumbling, but amazingly conditioned to obey their boss, no matter what, the cast drifted back to their rooms. Joe signaled for me to stand close so he could whisper. "I want you to listen carefully. This could ruin Surfside. Destroy everything we've worked for."

"My God! Is that all you can think about?"

He cut me off. "Just five performances left in our season. We're nearly sold out!"

"But what about . . . ?"

His tone turned menacing. "I don't know what went on between you and Frank and it's probably better that I never do. But, I think it's best if you spend the night in my room. Get your toothbrush and anything else you need and come down as soon as you can. The Sheriff will have a gazillion questions and I can help with your answers."

Too numb to muster a protest, I darted into my cubicle and avoided everyone's stares—especially Lisa's. Glancing into the little mirror on my nightstand, I had an urge to run from the house and hurl myself into the ocean. But fear of the police combined with how doing something that awful would affect my parents, kept me from trying it. Instead, I fell on my mattress and hoped the pillow was muffling my sobs. After a time, Maggie, the no-nonsense but kindly stage-manager, tapped on my door.

"Joe wants you downstairs, right away. He said to remind you to bring your overnight things." I grabbed my shaving kit, my towel, a change of socks and underwear and followed her.

Joe was just finishing up on the phone when we arrived at his door. "Thank you, Sheriff. That's very understanding of you. We'll see you shortly." He hung up and turned to face us. "Thank you, Maggie." He gestured for her to leave. "That will be all for now. Come in, Bob and close the door." A large, three-dimensional depiction of Christ on the Cross, hung over a roll-top desk, apparently the only ornamentation in his spacious, if spartan room.

"Take a seat there on the day bed. The ambulance will be here any minute," he said, assuringly.

"What about the police? Won't they be here first?"

"Thank God Sheriff Bradley is a good friend of ours," Joe said, with a wink. "Here's the plan, and it mustn't go any further than this room, for now. Understood? Sheriff Bradley is directing the ambulance to rush Frank to the hospital on the mainland. Have them make the death pronouncement over there. He'll stay here with one of his men and write up his report. Tomorrow, he'll inform the *Beacon* and the *Beachcomber* that Frank suffered from a rare heart condition—which caused him to have a stroke and that's how he died."

"But that's a lie, Joe."

"A white lie. There's a difference. You've always had permission to call me Joe. But I think for the sake of appearances, tonight you'd better address me as 'Mr. Hayden' 'til we get through this."

"Alright, *Mr. Hayden*." I was choking back tears. "But I don't understand. It's obvious Frank hung himself—everyone in the company saw it."

"True." Joe reached to put his arm around me, but I was having none of it. "And Sheriff Bradley expects us to tell him everything we know about it. At the same time, we have to think of the bigger picture. For the sake of Surfside's image and all that we contribute to the island's tourism, a stroke is the better story."

"What about Frank's family? What are you going to tell them?"

"Doesn't have one. Frank was an orphan, remember?"

"Makes it even worse."

Shortly before midnight, the ambulance took Frank's body away. I heard them but I couldn't bring myself to watch, even if Joe had allowed me to. Sheriff Bradley's interrogation was gentle and sympathetic after he confirmed that everyone except Frank had been at the theatre rehearsing all day and evening and no alibi's were needed.

I have no idea how any of us got through that night, but somehow, we did. When I later heard that several cast members had slept on the beach, I experienced a moment of anguish, wondering if anyone had used my comforter.

At the start of rehearsals Wednesday morning, Joe led us in a fervent prayer for God's blessing and Frank's salvation and followed it with a reworking of one of his legendary pep-talks. "Enthusiasm! Enthusiasm! Enthusiasm! That's the motto for the day, people. That's the secret of our success for *Rumpelstiltskin* this afternoon and our tribute to Weill and Berlin tonight. Nothing lifts an audience up like a performer brimming with *Confidence* and *Enthusiasm* and flashing a *Big Smile*. All great stars of the stage share that quality—unbridled enthusiasm. The show must go on! The show will go on! The show does go on! I know in my heart just as you know it in each of yours—Frank Albany would not have wanted it any other way."

Eyes rolled and chagrined looks were exchanged. Obviously, none of us knew how Frank felt about anything, but there was no stopping Joe's mania for theatrical platitudes.

"Bob, you're going to replace Frank as the Dancing Cobbler in "Rumpelstiltskin" this afternoon. Louise will simplify the choreography—she'll make it nice and easy, for you, won't you dear? I'll run the dimmer boards during that scene."

"Oh, my God," Lisa groaned. Is that really necessary, Joe? We're all still in shock and . . ."

"Yes it is, Lisa. All part of the 'the show must go on' credo. What better time to join together and experience that timeless tradition? I suggest you concentrate on your interpretation of 'My Ship' and find a way to knock 'em outta' their seats tonight."

"I am. I am. But I'm not wearing another one of those damned tube tops. I bought a Chinese silk blouse at Gerber's—with my own money and I'm wearing it instead!"

Happily, her little defiance seemed to ease the pall. Several cast members laughed aloud, especially the girls who shared Lisa's loathing for the unflattering tops.

Joe ignored her insubordination and plunged on. "Since there's no next of kin or immediate family, the County Coroner will probably order that Frank be cremated and we'll be given his ashes. We'll scatter some of them on our stage and the rest on the beach. You know how much he loved the beach."

This was greeted with gasps followed by a horrified silence. Too numb to comprehend the magnitude of Joe's insensitivity, I raised my hand for permission to leave, but Joe gestured for me to sit down. He had one more jolter for us. "I've decided to dedicate the final performances to Frank which I'll do over the sound system just before the overture, then, during curtain calls, you all will take up a collection for a scholarship in his name."

"What kind of scholarship?" someone asked.

"A Surfside apprenticeship, of course," he replied. "What else? Now, let's get to work, people. Chop, chop! Everyone pull together. If we work this right, I feel a standing ovation coming on."

As predicted, the audience gave us a standing ovation every night that week, though I suspected Joe had planted the idea in the heads of the season-ticket regulars. Who can resist joining a half dozen grandmother and grandfather types applauding while struggling to their feet in the front row?

Lisa surprised everyone with the gut-wrenching pathos she brought to the famous lyrics, 'My ship has sails that are made of silk, The decks are trimmed with gold.' By the time she broached the final chorus, most of the seniors were weeping audibly.

"If the ship I sing, Doesn't also bring, My own true love to me."

Such was the magic of live theatre, or so I believed—all too briefly, as it turned out.

Frank's funeral mass was held at *Holy Mother By The Bay* on Saturday afternoon. In the absence of a casket, Joe insisted I reframe one of Frank's black and white glossies from the lobby display and mount it on an easel. As a non-Catholic, I wasn't allowed to step foot on the altar, but when I handed it to Father Anzelm, the Polish priest down from South Philadelphia for the summer, he surprised me by asking for my opinion on its placement. Almost the entire company was in attendance, along with a dozen or so audience regulars. Claiming her grief was too intense, Louise begged off, as did Lisa, who had volunteered to console her.

Sunday night, as we were packing—most everyone was anxious to leave on the first bus Monday morning—Lisa tapped on my door. "We need to talk, but not here," she insisted.

"Not now, Lisa. Got to finish packing. My parents are picking me up in the morning, taking me back home for a few days. I'm breaking the news that I've decided to move to New York and take my chances. They're not going to like it."

"I really think we should talk now." The edge in her voice was palpable. "Only take a few minutes."

"I just told you—I should be in the city by next weekend. You gave me your phone number. I'll call you after I arrive and we'll get together."

"I wouldn't be in such a rush to get to New York, if I was you." She made no effort to hide her agitation. "Besides, I'll probably be out of town by then. Some college outside Boston is doing "Lady In The Dark" and lost their leading lady. Somebody told them about me and they called my Mother."

Ignoring her sinister tone, I elaborated, "Joe says it's never too early to strike while the iron is hot."

"Joe is not the big wheel he wants everyone to think he is," she snarled. "What does he know? Off the island—he's just another half-baked fru . . . a nobody."

"That's not very nice, Lisa. He's been especially kind to me, to all of us. Promised to help me find a room in New York, maybe an apartment to share—all that kinda' stuff."

Furious, she stepped between me and my suitcase and raised her voice. "I don't think this can wait another goddam minute."

"Lisa, please? Get out of my way and let me finish packing."

She didn't move but began to swat at me like a tigress protecting her cub's supper. "I knew it! I knew all along *you* were one of those goddam queers," she snarled. "But Frank—he fooled me. I never would have guessed—and you can bet Louise never did, either. Frank talked so high and mighty about being a good Catholic—told Louise he was saving it until he got married. Saving what? 'Til he did what? What a crock! I saw you two screwing on the beach that night!"

Several cast members gathered at my door, their faces creased in disbelief.

"Nor was I the only one who was out on those dunes," she raved on. "No Siree, not the only one."

"Lisa, hold on," Dimitri, the drummer, urged. "This is not the time or place for . . ."

But there was no stopping her. "I swore not to say a word to anybody but it was all I could do not to tell Louise, as it would have broken her heart. First Frank turned her down and then she went after you and you ignored her! And, to think I had the hots for you, too. What a sap. How dumb can two straight girls be? Pretty goddam dumb, apparently."

Joe pushed his way through the gathering. "That's enough, Lisa. Why don't you come with me? We'll go out on the back deck. Drink a Coke or something."

"I hate Coke! Everybody knows that. You fairies are all alike," she screamed. "Always leading everybody on." She slapped me across the face with such force she broke off a finger nail which lodged in my left cheek. So shocked was everyone, it was several moments before Joe and Maggie could grab Lisa's arms and hold them behind her. "Now look what happened!" she raved on. "I hope it was worth it."

"We need to get her to a hospital right away," Maggie declared.

"All of you—hold her down," Joe said, with remarkable calm, "While I call an ambulance."

But Lisa wasn't finished just yet. "If being a fag is such a great thing, why do so many of you end up killing yourselves?"

Dimitri led me to the bathroom, carefully removed the fake nail from my cheek and daubed the cut with iodine.

Minutes later the emergency squad arrived, buckled Lisa in a straitjacket (the first one I'd ever seen) and administered a syringe that brought instant calm. When they asked her to lie down on the gurney, she responded in a fuzzy voice, "Last February I played Stella in "Streetcar" at the West Orange Playhouse," she bragged to the youngest medic. "In the play, her sister, Blanche has that famous line at the end—when they're takin' her away to the looney bin? 'I have always put my trust in the kindness of strangers.' Lisa tilted her head and glared straight at him. "You won't mind if I put my knee in your nuts, instead?" Fortunately, the female medic was quicker than Lisa and had her flattened on the gurney before she could accomplish it.

I saw Lisa only one time after that—a couple of years later at an open-call for a bus and truck company of "Flower Drum Song." I'd come along with an Asian-American actor-friend, not to audition, but to lend moral support. It was he who first spotted Lisa and was rightly appalled by how she'd tricked up her eyes. To achieve an oriental look, she'd placed surgical tape over her eyelids and pulled them into crude slits. If she recognized me that afternoon, and there was no reason why she couldn't, she made a point of avoiding all contact. When I sensed her game, I did the same.

As I crossed the country, every painful detail of this long-buried story came back to me, complete with sensory perception. The recollection of that terrible final week on the island came into full focus just as we were landing at JFK. That evening, attending the brilliant musical, "Light In The Piazza" at Lincoln Center helped put it out of my mind. But not for long.

Next morning, walking past the newsstand outside my hotel, I spotted this headline, and immediately bought a copy:

BLACK WIDOW STUNG AT LAX

Exclusive to NY Post, April 21, 2004

An elderly woman, who the DEA has dubbed "The Black Widow" was arrested at LAX early yesterday morning as she attempted to board a flight to JFK. Identified as Lisa M. Fontanne, the 77 year old woman claimed to be a modern dance choreographer en route to a DanceAmerica Forum at the 92nd St. YWCA. She was being routinely screened by airport security when small amounts of what appeared to be heroin and cocaine were found on her skirt and hair piece, **Sgt. Jim Holcomb** told the Post. "She was arrested at about 7:30 am and remains in our custody."

A search of her luggage and person produced 6 kilograms of cocaine taped to her abdomen, 4 pounds of marijuana stowed in her bra, several zip baggies, party balloons and condoms found in her carry on bag, contained heroin and cocaine and a vitamin tray was packed with more than 200 tabs of Ecstasy and Oxycodone.

It's believed her clients were mostly wealthy retirees on New York's Upper East & West Side.

Known by her neighbors for her all-black fashions and her frequent renditions of 'My Ship" from the 1941 Kurt Weill musical, "Lady In The Dark," Ms. Fontanne (The Black Widow) has heretofore been regarded by the authorities as merely eccentric, but the recent increase in airport security measures forced the DEA to take a closer look at the elderly and wheelchair bound.

Ms. Fontanne, listed as residing in South Central Los Angeles, is being held on a $1.5 million bond.

The Astor Twins

So unexpressive were their faces, so identical their hair and skin color, so unremarkable their conversation, none of their neighbors nor anyone in their immediate acquaintance had ever succeeded in figuring out their ages, ethnic background or how to tell them apart. Because neither woman ever referred to her heritage or hometown, it was assumed these subjects were off limits to any but their closest associates. Such taboos conjoined to make them the object of ongoing curiosity and earned them a begrudging admiration from everyone within a four block radius of their Vermont Avenue apartment building.

Despite faded photos of the girls book-ending Red Skelton at a clown painting exhibition for charity in 1951, and rumor that they'd alternated as the Avon Lady in that firm's first TV commercials, their sketchy resume was virtually unverifiable. Their caterpillar eyelashes, preposterous Mae West wigs and sequined pant-suits, made Maizie and Mitzi Astor an object of derision, but nevertheless, one that deserved respect.

Strict instructions were imparted to any and all, prior to being given an introduction. "For heaven's sake, don't ask their age or where they come from," Hervé Limon would caution in an urgent whisper as he approached their red-lacquered, badly chipped door. Hervé, a rotund and jovial Panamanian, himself of indeterminate age, tripled as the twin's personal manager, make-up and hair consultant and major domo, and had done so for nearly two decades while moon-lighting as maintenance man for *La Sonnambula,* the time-warped, Tuscany Villa-styled apartment complex, nestled at that busiest of intersections on the hillside beneath the *Hollywood Sign* and the *Griffith Observatory.*

These introductions never came about casually, but were the result of considerable negotiation through the Twin's locked-door and the requisite bribe of a fifth of Glen Livit or Napoleon brandy discretely placed in Hervé's manicured hands, usually with the promise of an Avon Collectible to follow. The twins were well aware of this commerce, and it was assumed they received their fair share of the spoils, for celebrity, no matter how insular, fleeting or former, was still worth something in Hollywood, and they damned-well knew it!

"Ding Dong, Avon calling!" Maizie and Mitzi would sing out in chorus, before commencing to turn their four dead-bolts. "We hear you have a part for us," Mitzi would say. "Did you bring a script?" Maizie would ask, followed immediately by Mitzi's admonition, "We always work together and only accept above-the-title billing." Then together, "As a fellow pro, we know you understand."

This inevitably made for an awkward moment for the folks waiting in the hallway. Rarely, if ever, did these celebrity-seekers have any real connection with show-business. Those clamoring for an audience with the Twins might include a newly arrived (via Trailways or Greyhound) aspiring actor or actress, but more often it was a retired Riverside County couple on self-guided holiday, hell bent for a photo-op with some kind of celebrity before returning home. Add in the occasional professor of TV history from Upstate New York or an avid Avon Collectibles couple from the mid-West, and you have a pretty good picture of the madding crowd clamoring to meet the Astor Twins, Vermont Avenue's self-described living legends.

The women had been buying and hoarding Avon collectibles since the early '60s when a catalogue first appeared in their mailbox. Its letter from the VP of Heirlooms read:

"Official" Avon collectibles are offered through the company and will include "Exclusive" or "first-to-market" items. These will come with certificates of Avon authenticity. They can also be branded or licensed products, numbered items such as Avon Steins, seasonal/sentimental dated items, or items designed exclusively, internally, by Avon. Certain to become a valuable addition to your family's estate.

Don't miss out! Start collecting now with our Glass Car Decanter!

By 1972, the Astor's collection of glass and plastic Pot Bellied Stoves, French Telephones, Golf Carts, Canadian Geese, Bishop Chess pieces, Indian teepees, Courting Roses, Fire hydrants, Juke Boxes, Pony Posts, Paddle-Wheeled Steamships and Covered Wagons had grown so out of control, they were forced to make a decision. Either put it in storage, sell it at a yard sale (alas, La Sonnambula only had a tiny back patio) or sign a long-term lease on an adjoining one-bedroom apartment. They chose the latter and with Hervé's enthusiastic help, began installing all manner of shelves, cabinets and knickknack stands to display their hundreds of cunning figurines, ornaments, plates and steins, with little thought for dusting requirements or earthquakes.

The finishing touch came when Hervé mounted a needlepointed sign over the newly created opening leading from their broom closet into the adjoining apartment: *Musée des Verres d'Avon. Accès $3.50 Exact Change Appreciated.*

One of the most admired areas in their collection was the étagère bearing an assortment of men's colognes in the shape of firearms. These life-like, life-sized replications included a Philadelphia Derringer, a Volcanic Repeating Pistol, a Pepperbox Pistol and a '20 paces pistol' presumably for use in after-shave dueling.

The Philadelphia Derringer had once been put to use by the Twins to scare away an intruder attempting to make off with their prized collectible and star attraction, the shaft-shaped men's cologne called *'The Defender Cannon.'* Though children under 16 were never admitted into the collection unless accompanied by Hervé and at least one responsible adult, it was decided in an abundance of caution, to display the Defender Cannon on the highest shelf, where it reposed in its original velveteen presentation box.

The first edition of 'The D. C." as it was affectionately referred to by its Hungarian designer, became an instant sensation and proved wildly popular among women of all ages. The men's cologne container sold out so quickly, it motivated the marketing directors at Avon to commission a study initially directed at military wives. However, the results were so startling, the company decided to bury them, and quickly. The survey revealed that the Cognoscenti of collectibles referred to it as the 'Avon Marital Aid,' but the less refined had dubbed it 'The Avon Dildo.' Maizie and Mitzi, amateur observers of Czarist Russian history, had early on named it 'Rasputin.'

Hervé had a cousin named 'Panama' Hattie Wu who managed the Burning Sands Molded Glass Plant down in Placentia, where much of Avon's sub-contract work was executed. When word of the marketing survey leaked to Panama, she immediately called Hervé, knowing of the Astor Twin's Musée and his relationship to it. Together they sensed, even if the Avon executives didn't, that the Defender Cannon, in the right hands, could be pure gold. The trick was to make the intriguing little bottle seem scarcer than it was and within a half hour they hatched a plan that would give them both a measure of financial security for the rest of their lives.

In a matter of days, Panama had set up molding ovens in an abandoned Laundromat behind the Jehovah's Witness Tabernacle in nearby Garden Grove. Simultaneously, Hervé set about getting every fundamentalist and born-again he knew to write letters to Avon, complaining about the obscene and overtly pornographic design of the collectible. Results of his machinations were immediately apparent, as the cologne cannon became harder and harder to lay hands on.

All the while, Panama and her band of hardy illegals were turning them out as fast as they could be cooled with Vaseline and tinted water and mailed to neighborhood porn and fetish shops, sans cologne, for the wholesale price of $9.95 per unit, plus shipping and handling. Retail prices started at $29.95 for the standard size and ranged all the way up to $49.95 for the 'Kong'.

Hervé, as erstwhile custodian of La Sonnambula, had keys to the basement and its vast storage cages, which he filled with thousands of cannons, concealed in boxes marked "House Xmas Decs." Throughout the 70's and well into the 80's, their black-marketing of the faux cannons escaped Avon's scrutiny as well as the regulatory eye of the California Fair Trade Commission.

It wasn't until Hervé's untimely death, electrocuted by a faulty heating coil while attempting to shrink-wrap his own waist, that the Astor Twin's were forced to confront his years of deception. "Oh well, maybe ABC or Lifetime will make a TV movie out of our story," Maizie said, determined to put a shine on the grim situation, as was her nature.

"And we can play ourselves," Mitzie exclaimed.

"With above the title billing," added Maizie.

"It'll be called . . ."

They giggled and sang in chorus, "Ding Dong, Avon calling!"

Queen of the Chateau Marmont

"Hah! Geoffrey, it's me. I'm in my regular—fourth floor front. The one that used to have a great view of the Garden of Allah. Now it overlooks that goddam bank that keeps changing its name. Nazimova must be spinning in her grave. Great old broad, Nazimova, 'til not landing any decent parts made her crazy. Christ, what a business! Sinatra, cool it! You'll just have to wait 'til your Uncle Geoff gets here. So, how soon will that be, darling?"

"Rachelle?"

"How many broads do you know with a pooch named Sinatra?"

"Thanks for the heads up. How long have you been in town?"

"Don't be stupid! You know how these things go." She held the receiver away to cough. I could almost smell the tobacco tars over the phone. "My cockamamie agent, Michael 'Heartburn' set the deal late yesterday and I caught the early flight this morning. Blah de blah blah. So when do we see you?"

"What's the show?"

"Don't know. Haven't opened the script yet. It's a job that gets me out of the Pennsylvania cold. We'll have a few laughs. So when?"

"I'm stuck at the office for at least another two hours. How's 7:00?"

"Sinatra will be eating the rugs by then. I'll order something from room service to tide him over. Would you mind picking up some Hartz Puppie Chow on the way? Those little cans he likes? Gristede's carries them."

"Gristede's is in New York, Rachelle. We have Ralphs out here and they carry all kinds of dog food."

"It's not just *any dog food*, goddam it! The only thing my boys will eat is Hartz Puppie Chow, so don't bother to bring anything else if you can't find it."

"Relax, I'm sure Ralphs will have it."

"Ralphs Schmalphs! What's with you and your goddam Ralphs?" Another rumbling cough. "We're almost out of Smirnoff, too. Get us a fifth. No, better make it one of those half-gallons. Saves a few bucks and keeps the boys at the front desk from blabbing to the Enquirer every time they see the delivery guy. Did I tell you, they finally fired that bastard assistant manager? The son-of-bitch was peddling information to every tabloid in town." She coughed again, this time long enough to alarm me.

"Rachelle, are you okay? That cough sounds pretty bad."

Whenever I commented on anything pertaining to her smoking, she ignored me completely. "Better pick up a carton of *Virginia Slims*, while you're at it. The brown ones with the gold tip. I'll pay you back when you get here. And what's with this 7:00 o'clock crap, bubbeleh? I thought you were the boss?"

"I am. That's why I have to stay here 'til closing." Even after all these years, Rachelle could put me on the defensive in a few short sentences. "I'll try to leave a little earlier," I added, lamely.

"Hah! That's my man! Show some balls. Sinatra will love you forever. Martin doesn't give a damn," and she slammed the receiver down. Happy or angry, Rachelle always slammed the receiver down. In all the years I'd known her, I've never seen or heard of her writing so much as a post card to anyone, so I figured slamming the phone down was her version of an exclamation point.

With my permission, Robbie, my assistant, had been listening in on his extension. His awe for old-time Hollywood stars reached its apogee with Rachelle and was totally disproportionate to his dislike for her two Pekinese, *Sinatra and Martin.* 'Snarling little shits,' was his uncharitable appraisal whenever she dragged them along to my office.

"I know the drill," he yelled from his cubicle in the back. "I'll run to Ralphs and get the vodka, cigarettes and dog food. First, pick up the intercom, Boss." When I did, he whispered in unctuous concern, "Don't forget, you're meeting Agnes Moorehead in her trailer at her ABC MOW tomorrow morning. You know how La Raven likes to keep you up 'til all hours. Especially when she thinks you're doing work for Miss Moorehead. By the way, we're out of petty cash. Fifty ought to cover it."

"Alright. And get me a bottle of Tums while you're at it. Jumbo size." Despite the large amounts of alcohol I consumed while trying to keep up with Rachelle, I never allowed myself to become seriously intoxicated around her. Yet, the next morning, I inevitably experienced nausea accompanied by fierce stomach cramps, hence the Tums. "Thanks for your help, Robbie." I handed him the cash and returned to the stack of press releases, blind items and phone messages awaiting my attention.

So began a typical visit to the Chateau Marmont with the famously feisty actress whose face many people thought they recognized, but whose name only a few could recall. In later years, much to her amusement, Rachelle was often mistaken for Bette Davis—even after Davis was dead. "I wish I had her dough," she growled to the wide-eyed autograph seekers, then signed Davis' name with a giggle and a flourish.

I first saw Rachelle Raven when I was 15 years old during one of my early forays to New York. She'd recently replaced Jessica Tandy in the two character drama, *The Wedding Bed.* I remember registering disappointment when I realized I wasn't going to see the legendary Miss Tandy, famous for having played 'Blanche' in the original *Streetcar Named Desire,* opposite Marlon Brando. Still, the name Rachelle

Raven freighted glamour and theatricality in its euphony and I recovered.

My first impression of her, enhanced by wrinkle-softening footlights and the caché of a Broadway theatre, is preserved in amber. I recall her as being strikingly beautiful, surprisingly petite, and a proficient if icy-mannered actress. Yet, her performance, after such a long run, was anything but the mechanical contrivance one might expect. Despite her steely reserve, there was a spontaneity and winsomeness about her that left an indelible impression.

A few years later, I chanced to meet her co-star, Reginald Crawford, at his Greenwich Village co-op, and when I gushed about one of my first Broadway experiences was seeing him and Rachelle acting together, Crawford rolled his eyes.

"I'm surprised you survived to tell the tale," he sniffed. "I almost didn't. I was counting the days by the end of the run." He tapped his unfiltered cigarette on the kitchen stove and leaned down to light it off one of the burners. "Lord Dunhill is in hospital for a facelift," he explained and inhaled deeply. "Neither Rachelle nor I ever missed a performance. Not one. Even during the flu season. Positively drove our understudies crazy." He eyed me, quizzically, as if to gauge what I could handle.

"We were lovers, you know. But not for long. She wore me out." He inhaled again. "Not from fucking, mind you," he assured with clipped Cowardian diction. When I didn't ask for clarification, he shrugged and continued: "Rachelle hated to go to bed. Loved all-nighters with her good friend, Comrade Vodka. She could drink a Cossack under the table. Still can, they tell me." He glanced in the Empire-framed mirror hanging over the stove, and winked at me. "She never understood why some of us needed our beauty sleep."

A decade later, shortly after I'd given up my pursuit of an acting career and hung out my first Press Agenting shingle, I was surprised to receive a call from Reginald Crawford. Seems he'd heard from Rachelle recently and she was going through a rough patch. This was not to be repeated but the IRS was pursuing her for unpaid taxes on long-spent income; she hadn't had an offer for a movie role in years, had appeared in a succession of short-lived Broadway flops and was surviving on summer stock tours, suburban dinner theatres and Pennsylvania's penurious Unemployment Benefits.

According to Crawford, she wanted to make a fresh start and 'get her name out there with a new slant on it.' If I might be interested in representing her, he offered to arrange an introduction. Before I could answer, he said, "I don't know how much of a retainer you're asking for, but if you could be flexible, you and Rachelle might do each other 'a bit of alright' as my West End brethren are fond of saying."

"Sounds like a plan," I enthused. "Tell Miss Raven I'd be honored. And thank you for thinking of me, Mr. Crawford. Just say when and where."

"It's Reggie to you, dear Geoffrey. Always has been. Always will be. We'll be in touch."

My first office, located on West 44th Street, was a one room wonder, not much bigger than a one-star hotel suite, barely enough space for me and my part-time secretary to turn around in. Since the building had yet to paint my name on the door, I hoped that first meeting with Miss Raven could take place elsewhere. 'Sardi's would be nice,' I imagined, though I shuddered at the expense. 'Maybe Reggie would invite us to his place in the Village?'

That was just prior to my first glimpse at how Rachelle Raven operated, once she'd set her mind to it.

It was a Monday morning shortly before noon—my guy-Friday had swapped his day off to attend a friend's funeral. Manny, the garrulous but-not-too-swift maintenance man, banged on my door and stuck his head in. "Yo, Putnam. There's some old broad ridin' up and down the elevator, lookin' for ya'. I told her this was your office but she didn't see no sign or nothing and wanted me to make double sure."

"Good Lord, Manny. Did you get her name?"

"No, but she looks like she might be somebody, so I didn't wanna' ask."

"Well, where is she now?" I asked in a panic.

"The old broad is right here," a husky voice reverberated around the hallway.

"Miss Raven! What a surprise! Forgive me. I had no idea . . ."

"Of course you didn't. That's the whole point. I hate fancy-shmancey—all that bowing and scraping. This way I get to see what you're really like." She pressed a $5. bill into Manny's hand. "For your trouble, Manny. Next time this old broad shows up, you'll know where to bring her."

Manny removed his golf cap and bowed low. "Thank you, M'am. Real kind of you, M'am. Real kind."

"That will do for now." She waved him away. "We'll ring when we need you again."

Flustered and embarrassed, I commenced to babble. "I moved in just a month ago and haven't had time to do much with the place, except work, work, work. I'm afraid you'll have to sit in my secretary's chair, if you don't mind?"

"Long as it doesn't wrinkle my ass," she teased. Mistaking a vase for an ashtray, she took out a pack of Salems. "Hope you don't mind if I smoke. If you do, it could be a deal-breaker." Before I could answer, she lighted up and began puffing away.

"Let's cut to the chase. Reggie tells me you're a comer. Says you've got ethics *and* moxie—unbeatable combination." She stood to pace about the room, studying my books, stacks of newspapers and magazines and paused at a pair of framed theatrical posters inherited from my Great Uncle Wilbur in Jersey—as in 'Isle of', not 'New.' (Editor's note: remember that diploma from Shamokin Dam, PA)

"First, I need to find out if I can afford you—what kind of retainer you're expecting."

"Well that's readily negotiable, Miss Raven. It's more important to see how we fit. I'm a long-time fan of yours—so that ought to make my work . . ."

She cut me off. "Save the flattery for later. How much?"

"How's $50. a week, to start? Payable one month in advance."

She shook her head. "Not what I had in mind," she said and continued to study the *"Lady Windermere's Fan"* poster. "Art nouveau. Beautiful! I always wanted to play that role." Then she turned to me. "I'm prepared to offer you $75. a week. Let's give it six months and after that . . . we'll see."

"That's very generous, Miss Raven. Very fair."

She extended her hand. "No need for a contract. A handshake is better than paper—and think of all the trees it saves." We shook—her grip was surprisingly firm. "Now, you may call me Rachelle—in private of course. But never Rache! I hate it."

"Thank you, Rachelle. May I ask, do you always make decisions this quickly?"

"I'm a great judge of character. That's why I've only had to divorce three of my husbands." She guffawed and ground out her cigarette.

"I'm honored. And looking forward to a happy association."

"Me too, Bubbeleh. Now lock up your office and give it a rest. They're holding my table at Sardi's. You can impress me with the thousand ways you're going to promote my new image—over a vodka martini and Vincent's divine crab cakes."

And so it began.

I was surprised by the positive reaction from most of the old-guard columnists at the mention of Rachelle's name. Walter Winchell was the first to print a lengthy item. 'Stage and screen veteran, Rachelle Raven, is about to publish her first book on the art of crocheting. "I was lousy at crosswords so I taught myself, between takes on the set," she claims. Though born on Philadelphia's Main Line, the sloe-eyed beauty was originally dubbed "The Jewish Geisha" by the flacks at RKO. Still petite and glamorous, Rachelle is pouring through scripts as fast as they arrive at her Bucks County home. "Looking for just the right thing," she assured this long-time fan. "But it ain't easy, Walter." Hope you're listening, David Merrick. And break a leg, Rachelle.'

Soon after, Leonard Lyons, Earl Wilson, Rona Barrett, Louis Sobol and Dorothy Kilgallen followed suit with similar puffs. The old adage that most people like to see a fallen idol get back on his or her feet, prevailed. Rachelle was pleased, and, while Broadway and Hollywood weren't exactly beating down her door, offers for guest roles on series TV began to come in fairly regularly. And with her good news, my reputation swelled proportionately. I was sought out by a brace of semi-name older performers who weren't quite ready to hang up their tap shoes, and it made for a tough time trying to evaluate which ones I thought I could really help.

However, from the outset, my unmentioned dream was to eventually move my little office to Los Angeles. The Broadway game, while exhilarating and artistic, could be financially and emotionally depressing with its rigid hit or miss, feast or famine tradition and often proved to be downright degrading. I longed for a world where the payoff possibilities were grander, more frequent and might offer a chance for continuity. Ergo, I'd concentrate on actors who worked mostly in film and television. And, as the TV commercial field was just hitting its stride—always looking for a pretty face to promote its soaps and cigarettes, I planned to put my paddle in that pond, as well. So, almost 3 years to the day of my hand-shake with Rachelle, I invited her to lunch and broke the news that I'd be heading West in the late Spring.

"Ah, the old 'palm trees are always palmier' syndrome. I can't say I'm surprised. Have you told any of your other clients?"

"Not yet. But since you were my first *and* my good luck charm, you deserved to be the first to know."

The waiter approached our table. "Beg pardon, Miss Raven, but the chef asked me to convey his apologies. The truck that delivers our seafood broke down in the Palisades this morning and Chefs had to take the crabcakes off the menu. Mr. Sardi sends his apologies, as well, and suggests you might like to try the shrimp croquettes—with his compliments."

"Remind Vincent I'm allergic to shrimp. They give me hives. I guess he forgot. Bring me another martini, instead. Make it a double."

"Of all days . . ." I winced.

"Bad news always comes in threes," she cautioned. "Next, they'll tell me they're taking down my caricature."

"I doubt that, Rachelle. It's right there, over your head."

"For now. Have you lined up any clients yet?"

"Yes, I have one star ready to sign and several others expressed interest in meeting with me, right after I get settled."

"Name one! And don't bullshit me, Geoffrey or I'll become very cross with you."

"Agnes Moorehead."

"Nukh a star! What's that old dagger need you for? She's got all the money in the world—takes every cockamamie job that comes her way. You know how many parts I've lost to her?"

"Craig Stevens and Alexis Smith."

Rachelle sputtered in her martini. "You're kidding, right?"

"No. Why would you think that?"

She took another big gulp. "Had 'em both . . ."

"Did you say what I thought you said?"

"Yes," she leered demurely. "Separately, of course."

"Dare I mention your name when I meet with them?"

"Suit yourself. They're both so cagey, they'll probably say 'Rachelle who?'"

"I doubt that. Everyone always wants to know who's on my current client list, anyway."

"I predict you're going to hate it out there. You'll see. Those West Coast queens can be very slippery about paying commissions and retainers."

"No worse than here in New York," a rich male voice intoned from behind us. It was John Springer, the acknowledged Dean of Broadway press agents. Handsome, charming, erudite, he was the dapper gentleman everyone wanted to be when they grow up. "Rachelle, what a happy surprise!" he said and bussed her on both cheeks. I thought I caught them exchanging a knowing look, but it could have been my intimidation.

"Life in the country must suit you," he gushed. "You look younger every time you come to town."

"John, there's no bigger flatterer than you—and no one who loves it more than I. This is my, soon to be *ex-press* representative, Geoffrey . . ."

" . . . Geoffrey Putnam, of course. I know you by reputation. And a good one it is—so far."

"It's an honor, Mr. Springer." I stood to shake his hand. "When it comes to reputations, I can honestly say that yours has been my inspiration."

"What is this?" Rachelle interjected. "A 'who-can-out-compliment-who' contest?" which made Springer chuckle and me blush. "John, you'll join us for a drink, won't you?" she asked.

"Afraid I can't, darling. I'm with Celeste Holm and Romney Brent. They've been approached by Lawrence Langner about doing something with the Guild and they wanted my two cents."

"How nice," she purred and turned to blow a kiss. "Do tell Celeste and Romney how happy I am for them," she added, masking any hint of envy.

"I will do that, dear lady. And here's my card. Don't hesitate to call if I can be of help in any way. Nice to meet you, Geoffrey. Good luck on all your future endeavors."

"Wasn't that dear of him?" she murmured as she tucked his card in her décolletage.

"Yes, but why does this feel like a set-up, Rachelle?"

"It's a small world, Bubbeleh. Word gets around very fast."

"So you knew before I invited you to lunch?"

"Of course. I heard it a week ago, from the boys in the box office at the Bucks County Playhouse."

"Well, shut mah mouth, Miz Raven." I think it's time I had a Martini. Oh, waiter?"

To call our parting 'bittersweet' is putting poetry where none was, but, to our credit, we didn't go after each other with forked tongues, an all too common practice when fiduciary and artist split. However, to my disappointment, Rachelle behaved like one of those iron butterflies who, once you've shifted total focus from them, are fairly done with you. Still, no ugly words about me surfaced, certainly none from me were said about her.

Over the ensuing years, Rachelle was awarded an Obie for her role in Albee's *The Sandbox*, nominated for a Tony for a short-lived revival of Tennessee Williams' *Milktrain;* two Emmy nominations for *Law and Order* and a Golden Globe and People's Choice nominations for a *Hallmark Hall of Fame*—none of which she won, but just being named made everyone who followed her career feel proud for her. From time to time, I would hear scuttlebutt that she'd clashed with a director over a line reading or a bit of dialogue; was struggling more and more to remember her lines and had viciously put down a fellow cast member—usually a female, much younger than herself, someone who was a quick study who had accidentally called attention to Rachelle's memory problem. Next day, she would order expensive flower arrangements to be delivered to the injured party. Her notes of apology became something of a collector's item:

> *"Dear_____, I'm over it. If you knew what these cost, you'd be over it, too. All is forgiven. Rachelle R."*

Years later we ran into each other on location for an NBC movie of the week. She was playing a feisty grandmother-hostage in a bank-heist film based on a true-life story. Within minutes, it was as if we'd never parted.

"John Springer did a brilliant job for me after you left town, Bubbeleh. I can't complain. But truth is, what the hell do I need a press agent for these days?" she asked rhetorically. Even in her late 70's, she could summon up glimmers of her sloe-eyed and flirty old self. "So maybe we could be friends again? What do you think, Geoffrey?"

"I never thought we stopped," I fibbed.

She stared at me, looking for a double meaning, then decided there wasn't one or she'd ignore it if there was. "Lately, I've been coming out here three or four times a year. They may call it 'the Boob Tube,' but long as they keep paying me my usual ten grand a week, put me up at the Marmont and let me drag my pooches along, I'm a happy camper."

"Nobody more deserving than you, Rachelle."

"Don't know about that, but the IRS bandits have finally returned to their caves—the mortgage on the house in New Hope is retired . . ."

"Life is good and even better when you're talented."

"No need to blow smoke up my ass, Geoffrey. So, what are you doing about dinner tonight? They say this director gets the martini shot by five-thirty. What do you say?"

"I'd like that, Rachelle. I really would."

Simple as that, she was back in my life—but without the stress of "What did you do for me today, Bubbeleh?" I'd visit her on the set, we'd meet for supper, tour L.A. County Museum on her day off. Her smoking continued non-stop, the vodka flowed more freely than ever, but Rachelle seemed to have mellowed and I must have, as well.

Shortly after checking into the Chateau, she would call me and exchange virtually the same dialogue each time: "Sinatra, cool it! You'll just have to wait 'til your Uncle Geoff gets here. So, how soon will that be, darling?"

"Rachelle?"

"How many broads do you know with a pooch named Sinatra?"

"Thanks for the heads up. How long have you been in town?"

"Don't be stupid! You know how these things go." And we were off to the races. That was our pattern for years—until her final visit.

That fateful night, I crossed the lobby, dutifully bearing a half-gallon of Smirnoff, a carton of Virginia Slims and six cans of Hartz Puppy chow. I'd been doing this for so long, the front desk clerk barely looked up when he waved. "Nice to see you, Mr. Putnam," he called out. The elevator man from Auckland glanced at my bags and bid, "Good evening, Sir. I assume we're headed to Miss Raven's on four?"

She was waiting for me in the doorway, resplendent in an embroidered red-silk kimono, black silk pedal-pushers and a long cigarette holder.

"What's with the Cho Cho San drag, Rachelle?"

"Don't be rude! You've seen it before. It's the one the producers gave me after the 'Auntie Mame' tour.

"All very lovely, but it's 52 degrees outside. 'Mame' will freeze her ass off."

"Slight change of plans, Bubbeleh. I've ordered take out from Chin Chin—their five course Mandarin sampler. Should be here any minute. Thought it might be fun to stay in for a change."

"Okay, but I'd better cancel Musso and Franks."

"No need. I had Robbie do it already. He said you have an early call in the morning—the special effects people are coming here to fit me for a prosthetic at 10, so everything ought to work out nicely."

"What kind of a prosthetic?"

"It'll make it look like there's a hole in my head. And no wise-assed remarks about it being a redundancy."

"My, oh my! All that and Chinese from Chin Chin?" I laughed. "Who could ask for more?"

"Exactly! I'll pour us a drink while you look around the kitchen for a can opener. The boys are starving and those Hartz pull-off lids are hell on my nails."

She floated about the suite, lost in her 'Mame-as-geisha' incarnation, lighting a half-dozen emergency candles which she'd placed in ice-tea glasses. I spooned the dog-food into Sinatra and Martin's bowls and determined not to make comment.

Minutes later, the take-out arrived in the care of a high-strung young man who begged us to forgive his English as he'd recently emigrated from Croatia. Rachelle thought he was cute and insisted I give him a big tip. She arranged the containers on the dining table next to the window with the unrivaled view of Washington Mutual, poured us each another vodka and we proceeded to gorge in faux-Oriental splendor.

"Geoff, Bubbeleh, I got to thinking about something on the plane today. Don't laugh, but what do you think about helping me write my autobiography? What's that cockamamie thing they call it—'ghosting'?"

"You mean 'ghost-writing.' 'Ghosting' is what vaudevillians used to do to save money by doubling up in hotel rooms."

"Whatever. Everyone keeps nagging me, especially those decorator queens, you know, my neighbors in New Hope."

"Writing an autobiography is a tall order, Rachelle. Involves setting up a schedule—regular taping sessions—*discipline.* Digging deep . . ."

"What the hell you think I've been doing all these years?" she snapped. "They wanted happy—I gave them happy. They wanted tears, I gave 'em tears—sometimes for eight or nine takes. She lit up another Slims and poured another vodka. "This 'digging real deep' crap is for amateurs. Either you know how to act or you don't. No amount of naval-gazing can replace real talent."

Despite the sharpness of her rebuke, I sensed she was auditioning for me—to prove how cooperative she could be. After a contemplative silence, she sighed, "My biggest worry is nobody will give a good goddam."

"That's silly, Rachelle. Look at the life you've led? If you tell your story with candor and courage—combine it with a sense of humor about yourself, how can you miss?"

"You think so? Speaking of humor, I've wanted to ask you something about yours. Word got to me that you've named me one of your BCs? Is it true?"

"Well, yes, on occasion—but always behind your back." I winked, trying to gauge where she was going with this. "I don't know who spilled the beans, but I hope they told you it's something I call people who have a hard time accepting compliments. You certainly come under that category, Rachelle."

"What the hell is that supposed to mean?"

"BC is my version of a phrase they use in the English Theatre. Over there they say it as a compliment for talent and tenacity. It's not gender specific."

"I know perfectly well what the C stands for, Geoffrey. I did that movie with Hitchcock in Liverpool, remember? The crew used the C word all the time. It's the B that has me confused. Can't be *bitch.*"

"It isn't. 'B' stands for 'beloved.'

"Of course! 'Beloved Cunt!' Why couldn't I figure that out? Does that mean I'll be getting some kind of certificate?"

"No, but as the reigning Queen of all BCs, the BC Assulata, if you will, feel free to add the initials to your name at any time."

"Rachelle Raven, BC. I like it. Not so sure TV Guide will, but fuck 'em. They don't have to."

"I'm delighted that you're taking it as intended, Rachelle. Confirms my theory that most great artists have a tough time accepting a straight forward term of endearment."

"Don't push your luck, Bubbeleh. Now, what about my autobiography?"

"It's not something we should discuss while heavily cocktailed," I replied.

"Bullshit! Some of my best work happened when I had a couple of shots before they called 'Action.' Same thing on Broadway. How else do you think we faced those god-awful theatre party ladies on matinee days? Writing a book has to be a piece of cake, after that."

"It's not the same, I promise you."

"Come on. With my 'BC' mouth and your gift for blowing smoke—what's to lose?"

"You're incorrigible." I threw up my hands. "Let me see if Robbie stuck a notepad in my briefcase."

"You don't need to write anything down yet, Hemingway. That can wait 'til later. If it's important, you'll remember it."

"Rachelle, if you want this to work, you'll have to let me do my part my way."

"Alright, but don't ask me for dates. I'm lousy at remembering dates. I don't think in chronological order. I'll just say stuff as it comes to me. Go to the Motion Picture Academy and sort out the boring calendar details later."

"Sounds like you've given this some thought."

"Maybe I have." She put out her hand. "So, do we have a deal?"

"I guess—certainly for this evening. Where do you want to start."

"First shake my hand, Bubbeleh. No better way to prime the pump."

We shook and I produced a fresh tablet and a pair of sharp pencils. I've always preferred pencils over pens for everything except signatures. Rachelle poured another vodka, tamped out her barely-smoked Slim and lighted another. "So, where should I begin?" she asked as Sinatra and Martin vied for position in her lap.

"You said you wanted to freeform it—so freeform away. I'll only interrupt when I sense you're blatantly improvising or skirting around something important."

"All well and good, but I don't think much about this trend where old broads write about every graphic detail that took place in their bedrooms. What ever happened to leaving something to the imagination?"

"We'll work around that—but there's no avoiding the fact, sex sells. Look at Evelyn Keyes' book . . ."

"That's just what I'm talking about. What'd she call it? *Sister of Scarlett,* or something stupid like that?"

'*Scarlett O'Hara's Younger Sister."* What she revealed about her relationships with men, especially her marriage to Arte Shaw, that's what sold the book."

"What a shmuck! Arte Shaw would fuck a snake! Bastard—look what he did to Samantha Garden, for Christ's sake! She was what? Fourteen at the time? That other putz, Louis B. Mayer had to call in a ton of favors to keep Shaw out of jail."

"Should I be writing this down?"

"How the hell do I know? I've never done this before."

"Mentioning Louis B. Meyer seemed to get you steamed."

"Mayer was the meanest SOB in the business. Promoted that sanctimonious family-man crap to the public but in private he was a lecherous old needle-dick. What he put his starlets through! He'd threatened to cancel their contracts just to get a blow job. I'll never understand how Irene, his daughter, ended up being one of the nicest dames in the world. When Mayer found out about Garden and me, he . . . oh shit. Now look what you've done."

"I missed that last part," I fibbed. "I'd better take a fast course in shorthand, unless we use a tape recorder next time. Forgive me, you were saying?"

"Oh hell, why not? It's the one story I've never told anyone. Anyone who's still alive, that is. Maybe it's time to set the record straight." She extended her glass, as a Princess to her Handmaiden. "This will need freshening before I can say any more."

"If waiting on you is part of the deal, we'd better renegotiate right now."

"Oh don't be a bore, Bubbeleh. Just pour."

"Alright, but you're on your own, after this. Not only does Her Highness have an amazing capacity for liquid refreshment, but her humble servant has observed, she never seems to need the bathroom. How does she do it?"

"That's not funny! That's vulgar! And tacky! I'm surprised at you! A real lady knows how to hold her booze *and* her water, Mr. Potty Mouth."

"Consider handmaiden properly chastened," I sniggered as I bowed and placed the refill in her hand. " . . . if not totally humbled. Now, can Happy Scribe please get on with taking down precious words?"

"Smart ass!" She nodded regally and took a big sip. "Like I said, I'm terrible with dates but it must have been sometime around '49. The studios were beginning to feel the impact of TV—everybody was running scared. But the PR guys at the majors still carried a lot of weight with the newspapers. A couple of phone calls and they could get all sorts of garbage buried or planted, depending upon the whims of their bosses. Not like nowadays. The bastards report on you every time you wipe your . . . nose."

"I hate to interrupt, Rachelle, but you're wandering all over the map. What's your point? Is there an oyster in this pearl?"

"Don't rush me, goddam it! I know Sam had been fired from "You Gotta Have Rhythm" some time before—and went to a clinic somewhere in the Northwest, for help kicking the drugs and the booze. When she finally returned to MGM, the bastards put her on probation and eventually cancelled her contract completely. Never made the slightest effort to buy her out—after the millions she'd made for them. Makes me sick just to think about it."

She paused to stifle an unrelenting cough, which continued throughout the evening. "I can't say it was a great time for me, either. I was between husband #2 and #3—maybe it was #3 and #4—who knows, but one of them thought I too, should be thinking about drying out and offered to pay for it—so long as he could pick the hospital. I was too frazzed to argue with him so next thing I knew, he checked me into Peter Brent Brigham in Boston. It's where anybody who was anybody went, at the time—that is, if they could afford it. God knows what it cost.

I remember a lot of ice-baths, at least two sessions with the shrinks every day, long walks around the grounds trussed between two bull-dagger attendants and, every time I turned around, forgive the pun, the doctors were shooting my toochis with a vitamin cocktail. At least, that's what they said it was. I hated every goddam minute of it. Bucolia and that much healthful living never did suit me. But, if you had any hope of getting out of there, you had to pretend you were in hospital heaven for fear someone on the staff would write you up and extend your stay."

She looked down at her dogs and frowned. "You two must be getting fat. Right now you're way too heavy for Momma. Excuse me, while I put the boys to bed." She cradled the dogs in her arm and vanished into the second bedroom, but kept on talking.

"I'd been there about a week, when one night—I know it was after lockdown so it had to be late—yes, they actually locked us in our rooms at night—I heard the sound of someone crying—sobbing uncontrollably, really. It was coming from close by—if not next door, certainly from somewhere in the same wing. At the time, it struck me as the saddest sound I'd ever heard, made more so because there was something distinctively musical about it." With that, Rachelle stopped abruptly.

I'd been making notes as fast as I could and when I looked up, tears were running down her cheeks. "Take your time, Rachelle. It's a wonderful story. You got my attention right off."

"I'm not sure this belongs in the book. I mean, what's the point? It's all blood under the bridge. It's possible it could hurt someone, and I don't . . ."

"Look at what you're doing, Rachelle. We haven't officially started anything and already you're censoring yourself. Just tell your story. Leave the editing to me. We'll deal with the overall merit of each piece later."

She grabbed a tissue, blew her nose noisily and stared at me accusingly with those legendary saucer eyes.

"I hate to remind you, Princess, but you're the one that said it would be a piece of cake."

"Oh, shut up. Must be awful being right all the time."

"It's tough, but someone has to do it."

She shot me her 'if looks could kill' look, and smiled. "I guess I'm ready to go on."

"That's my girl."

"Next day, the nurses and attendants—even some of the doctors were all atwitter. 'Samantha Garden's here! Samantha Garden's here! She checked in last night. Think she'll mind if we ask for her autograph?' That kind of drivel.

I'd met Samantha at studio functions over the years—we'd chatted and I was sure she'd remember me—so I asked my doctor if patients were allowed to visit each other.

Big mistake. He was all cough and phlegm and looked like he had a broom handle stuck up his ass. "We don't encourage that form of fraternization during treatment," was his answer. So I gave him the raspberry and kept on asking around. When nobody said yes, I contrived to bump into Sam as she was coming out of her first session with the shrink.

"I'm so sorry, Miss Garden," I said. "It's Rachelle Raven. We met several times at . . ."

"Oh, for God's sake Rachelle," she said. "I know I'm looking like the wrong end of a rhino but please cut out the

'Miss Garden' stuff. It's Sam." We shared a quick hug before the attendants could stop us and when they were leading her away she yelled to me, "How long you been in this dump?' which wasn't her wisest turn of phrase and I made a note to clue her in as soon as I could.

Next day, Ursula, the nicer of my two daggers—I think she'd seen me in a couple of movies—Ursula looked aside so Sam and I could have a moment. I said I thought we were both in for pretty much the same reasons and it would be easier on her if she just went with the flow. I'd find a way to visit her, if she'd like—maybe later that night.

"I'd love that," she said. "I don't have anyone to talk to and I'm sick of this place already. The doctors talk to me like I'm crazy, and I'm not. They say I can't even let me speak to my husband or baby for another week or so."

When the attendant signaled that was all the time she could allow and grasped Sam by the arm to lead her away, she started to weep. "Please, take your hands off me. I'm not fighting you nor I'm I going anywhere but where you tell me." Again she looked over her shoulder to ask the world, "They call this a cure?"

There's no place on earth where a little grease doesn't make the gears run smoother, so I placed a couple of twenties where I thought they'd do the most good, and voila, I was sneaked into Samantha's room around 9:30 that night. We hugged and kissed and carried on like school girls on their first sleepover—brushed each other's hair—I think we even traded lipsticks. She insisted she had to get out of Brigham before she really did go crazy. I felt exactly the same way and told her so. She kept repeating how grateful she was that I was there—that I was the only one in the whole place who could possibly know what her life was really like. Between bouts of laughter and tears she begged me to promise I would never leave without her. I agreed, but the big question was 'how'?

Then I remembered an old beau named Edgar Viertel whose family owned a big piece of the Ritz-Carlton and Sam remembered staying there once, while on a studio junket. If I could get word to Edgar—he might cut us a deal and we'd be able to hide out in grand style. Sam loved the idea because she was sure it was the last place on earth Mr. Mayer and her husband would be looking for her.

We made a pact to escape as soon as possible and didn't give a thought about what we would do for money—we'd worry about that later. Sam felt we should attempt it under cover of night. I said she'd seen too many Charlie Chan movies and suggested it would be easier by day, perhaps during one of our walks around the hospital grounds.

She begged me to spend the night, but I knew that would really be pushing our luck. The staff change happened just before midnight and I'd promised my truckers I'd be back in my own bed by 11:30. Sam seemed to want to play the aggressor when I was about to leave, so I let her kiss me long and hard. I cautioned her not to breathe a word to anyone—be brave for the next few days while I got everything arranged. "You're the best, Rachelle. You're the absolute best thing that ever happened to me," she said, over and over. "We're going to have such a good time at the Ritz, I just know it."

We got lucky the very next day. I put a call into the Ritz and within minutes, Edgar called me back. To his credit, he liked intrigue with the best of them—he was on board in a heartbeat and came up with the idea to kidnap us! Using a delivery truck from another of his family's businesses—*Back Bay Wines and Spirits*—I think it was called."

At this point in her recall, Rachelle contracted a fit of giggles which segued into a ferocious bout of coughing followed by hiccups. I ran to the kitchen for some water, but she wanted no part of it. "That stuff could kill you. Water's the worse thing in the world for hiccups! I'll be alright in a minute," she insisted and miraculously, she was. She gave me a big smile and resumed exactly where she'd left off.

"Believe it or not, it all went off without a hitch. Edgar drove the truck himself and parked it beside the rose garden. Although it was a warm day, Sam and I had convinced our duennas that we were feeling chilly, so they let us wear coats over our bathrobes. Sam and I were standing just a few feet apart, when Edgar flashed the headlights on the truck, which was our "go' signal. Sam announced that she'd seen the Bluebird of Happiness in one of the bushes and began to sing to it. I distracted my nurse by telling them I needed somewhere to pee—right away. Two of Edgar's warehouse men—big bruisers those guys were—Irish, of course—ran up to us yelling, "Hold it right there, ladies. You're both under house arrest. You're comin' with us." You can imagine the look on our attendant's faces!

The men scooped us up, fireman style and ran for the truck. Sam couldn't resist gilding the lily as they lifted us into the loading door. "Oh officer, there must be some terrible mistake," she cried out. "I'm not who you think I am." 'Oh, just shut up, Sam,' I told her. 'There's no cameras rolling, and besides, everyone has seen that movie already.'

After it was all over, Sam and I had fun making up headlines for the Globe. My favorite was, "Garden and Raven kidnapped by Back Bay liquor truck!" I mean, you could file titanium on the irony of that image, Bubbeleh."

With Rachelle's ability to turn her emotions on a dime, I never quite knew whether she was 'working the room' or being genuinely forthright, but what followed seemed real enough.

"Sam was so talented—possibly the most gifted singing-actress I've ever known, certainly among the best of our generation. But so fragile! So damaged! And insecure! I don't know how she survived the studio system. Mayer had her on diet pills before she was 12—then Uppers to get her through the 12 hour shooting days. Followed that with a steady supply of downers so she could get her 'beauty sleep.' Even more amazing, Sam had developed a fine intellectual curiosity, despite her catch-as-catch-can education in a goddam studio trailer!"

With that, I thought Rachelle was about to call it a night, but I was wrong.

"She spent her life looking for someone to love—and someone to love her back—in kind. No crime in that. So she and I had a wonderful, what? six—seven weeks at the Ritz. Edgar thought it would be funny to register us as the Gumm sisters, which he did, though Sam wasn't crazy about that idea. But talk about generous! Edgar let us sign for everything, including new outfits from the boutique in the lobby.

Of course we knew it couldn't last. Reality was always too painful for Sam. She was stuck in her girl-next-door image and could never shed it. And the time was fast approaching for me to stop burning my candles at both ends. We were at each other's throats throughout our last week together. Nothing we could do or say was right for the other one. We had our worst row on the day Edgar invited me to join him for supper in his suite, just the two of us. I figured it was his not-so-subtle way of having one of us 'sing for our supper,' no matter that Sam was the singer and I couldn't carry a tune in a bucket. I also hoped a little time away would give each of us time to cool off. After a wonderful meal, served next to a window looking out over the Common, it was an easy decision to spend the rest of the night with Edgar.

He never told me whether he was in on it or not, but, next morning, when I returned to our room, Sam was gone. She didn't leave a note, nor any indication of how she'd done it. She was simply gone—without a trace.

I was told later that when the MGM detectives had finally tracked her down, they'd flown her husband to Boston with orders to bring her back to Culver City—and fast. Mayer was beside himself with fury. Immediately had me blackballed at every studio in town. You'll recall, it was another decade before I worked in a movie. It was that independent—we shot it in New York, guerilla-style. Had so many titles, I've forgotten the name."

"Under The Knife," I volunteered.

"If you say so. I was told it won a couple of awards at the Film Festivals. So, after being one of the highest paid actresses in the biz I landed on the Subway circuit. Played "Life With Father" and "Oh, Mistress Mine" in all 5 boroughs. But, I'm not complaining. At least I was able to pay the rent."

A lengthy silence followed another coughing spell. When Rachelle resumed, the wistful quality in her voice was unmistakable. "Sam and I never spent another evening together. The consequences were just too painful—any such revelation would have been deadly for both our careers. I went to see her concerts at the Winter Garden . . ."

"The Shuberts called it, *Garden at the Garden*," I interjected. "And they couldn't count the box office receipts fast enough."

"What a memory you have! Then, I saw her again at the Greek and the Bowl—always sent her a telegram—occasionally flowers. I never got a thank you, but that was okay. That was okay . . ."

At this point, she yawned, pointedly. "Listen, Bubbeleh, I have an idea. I know you have a big day tomorrow. You've had nearly as much to drink as I have . . ."

For the record, I hadn't, but there was no arguing I *was* dead tired.

"I'm sick of hearing my own voice. The boys are asleep in their room so why don't you stay here on the day bed? It's very comfortable. There's a toothbrush and every kind of toilet article in the little bath."

After hesitating for a moment, I agreed that it made sense. We hugged, she disappeared into her bedroom and made a point of locking her door. I washed my face, brushed my teeth with the nifty paste the Marmont provided, stripped to my T and shorts and fell on the daybed. Realizing I'd need some kind of nightlight to find my way back to the bathroom, I got back up and turned on the overhead in the hallway. Finally, I set the alarm on the clock radio for 7:00 and in seconds I was asleep, though fitful it proved to be.

It seemed no time before I was awakened by Sinatra and Martin's barking. "What's with you guys?" I asked before smelling the smoke curling from beneath Rachelle's door. "Jesus Christ! What's going on!" I turned the knob, then remembered she'd locked it and nearly broke my shoulder trying to break it down. First thing that came to mind was she must have left a cigarette burning somewhere. When finally, the doorframe splintered, I stumbled into a room filled with dense, acrid smoke. She must have been reading, as the lamp on the nightstand was still burning. Apparently the curtains and comforter were fireproof, for only the carpet was smoldering—the source of all that smoke. I held my arm to my face and fought my way across the room to the French doors which I remembered opened onto a tiny balcony. They parted abruptly and sent a potted cactus smashing to the roof below, raining its shards across the ground floor atrium. Almost immediately, the bedroom phone rang. I couldn't locate it and ran back to the living room to pick up that extension. It was the front desk. "Is there a problem up there?"

"Yes, there is! Call 9/11. Call the Fire department, call an ambulance. Get them here as fast as you can!"

And they did. But even though all departments showed up in record time, it was too late. Rachelle was gone. Within minutes, the medics pronounced her dead from smoke inhalation.

The next few days will forever remain a blur. The police, the coroner, the funeral arrangements, the studio, the hotel management, everyone wanted answers, especially the press who, for the most part, were exceedingly kind and considerate. All this was followed by Rachelle's cremation and a hastily arranged memorial service.

Despite the rules against pets at Doheny Towers, I brought Sinatra and Martin to stay with me, and after a time of mutual grieving, they behaved as if they'd been mine all along. Finally, I was presented with Rachelle's ashes, a few of which I keep in a porcelain box, beneath the bust of David, in my study. The rest I conveyed to New Hope and scattered under the weeping willow in Rachelle's back yard.

Oh, I almost forgot, later on the morning after the fire, I discovered my favorite BC had left me the ultimate farewell memento—lipstick on my penis.

The End